WHAT PEOP

THE V

Andrew Cairns has written, quite literally, a bewitching novel, one that speaks to an underbelly which lies dormant in us all. *The Witch's List* bridges our world of convention, with that of a fabulous Twilight Zone, what may be true reality – a realm of magic and ultimate possibility. I recommend this book because, behind the smokescreen of simplicity, there lies a masked bedrock of extraordinary power.
Tahir Shah, author of *The Caliph's House* etc.

A highly entertaining account of a boy's journey – both physical and emotional – from youth to manhood. From school-days to university, and into the workplace, we follow our young protagonist, 'Sandy' as he strives to build a life for himself. Leaving his home in Dundee he gravitates south, to France and then West Africa. The jarring cultural changes, which Sandy encounters, are brought to life authentically. The characters met along the way are fully developed and I formed an attachment to the young Scot that kept me gripped throughout, as the story builds towards a jaw-dropping conclusion.
Gregor Ewing, author of *Charlie, Meg and Me* and *Bruce, Meg and Me*

The Witch's List is a book full of colours and darkness. It transports you into the turbulent world of Sandy Beech, a young man experiencing adulthood with spirit and curiosity. His attraction for exotic women will trap him into unsuspected adventures in Africa. Andrew Cairns has brought off a lively, captivating novel and a unique cultural experience for the reader.
Isabelle Richaud, author of *Men in the Mirror*

The Witch's List by Andrew Cairns is a real page turner. As soon as you start to follow the main character, a young bloke by the name of Sandy Beech, you want to know more about him and follow his path. It leads him from his Scottish home to a French university, and finally to Africa.

For a guy who favours exotic women, and who does not believe in witchcraft, it's a dangerous way to go. Despite the warnings given by a dying nun, Sandy marries a beautiful black girl, Rocky, and, after a few years of faltering happiness, follows her to her home country, the Ivory Coast, in the hope of winning her back. There, he will witness strange events and be the victim of a series of physical assaults that will leave him deeply wounded, physically and mentally.

What's really happened to him ? Does this black magic really exist? In this coming of age novel, written with wit and great emotional precision, Andrew Cairns creates a strange mixture of mystery, humour, horror and passion. Through the eyes of a young European, *The Witch's List* also depicts the discovery of a strange continent, and it's different set of rules and values.

A must-read, captivating and bewitching.

Jean-Christophe Manuceau, author of *Cocteau Twins: Des Punks Célestes* and *L'homme Sans Parapluie*

The Witch's List

The Witch's List

Andrew Cairns

COSMIC
EGG
BOOKS

Winchester, UK
Washington, USA

First published by Cosmic Egg Books, 2015
Cosmic Egg Books is an imprint of John Hunt Publishing Ltd., Laurel House, Station Approach,
Alresford, Hants, SO24 9JH, UK
office1@jhpbooks.net
www.johnhuntpublishing.com

For distributor details and how to order please visit the 'Ordering' section on our website.

Text copyright: Andrew Cairns 2014

ISBN: 978 1 78535 348 2
Library of Congress Control Number: 2015956003

A CIP catalogue record for this book is available from the British Library.

Design: Lee Nash

Printed and bound by CPI Group (UK) Ltd, Croydon, CR0 4YY, UK

We operate a distinctive and ethical publishing philosophy in all
areas of our business, from our global network of authors to
production and worldwide distribution.

CONTENTS

Introduction

"Once you're on the witch's list, you're as good as dead."

Commonly held belief in the Ivory Coast (and elsewhere in Africa, where witchcraft is still practiced).

Part I

Chapter 1

Witches and Warlocks

I didn't use to believe in witches. Not really. Of course, growing up in Scotland, there were always stories of witches and wizards, ghosts and ghouls, monsters and zombies and so on, but as in most 'civilized' western countries, such stories were mainly regarded as folklore; on a par with pixies and elves. You didn't really believe in them, they were just fairy tales. *Remember the stories?*

There was one, more 'serious' book on witches in our secondary school library though. And it freaked us all out a bit. It must have been one of the most browsed texts in there – due to its filthy pictures of witches performing various ceremonies – black masses and the like – naked! In most libraries there are some books with scuddy pictures, classed under erotic literature or art; even in the children's section there's always some big kid that's got his hands on the encyclopaedia and invites you over to show you a picture of the topless, tribal African woman. This one, 'Witches and Warlocks', was a non-fiction work, detailing very graphically, and very sexily we all thought, a range of witchcraft and black arts practices. It had somehow found its way into Saint Saviours' RC (Roman Catholic) school, despite the establishment being as staunchly Catholic in its syllabus and overall culture as it comes. It was in the reference section, on the religious books shelf, and I'm sure none of the teachers knew of its existence, much less its saucy content. The librarian was a rather dozy woman in her thirties, with short blond hair; always had her nose in some novel. I assume it was her that ordered a copy. She must have done it absent-mindedly, not really checking out its profane and pornographic content. Or maybe she was some kind of closest anarchist or rebel. Who knows?

My best friend at the time, Martin Cardosi, always one to lead me into mischief, showed me the book at one point; we must have been in second year, aged thirteen, hormones beginning to rage.

"Here, Sandy, come and check this out." He shoved the big tome into my hands.

I flipped through it, speechless, mostly just looking at the shocking pictures but taking in some of the vocabulary: black mass, pentagram, hex, coven, sect, orgy...

"I'd like to join one of those devilish sects, just to take part in the orgies," said Martin, grinning.

"Idiot! You'd probably go to hell."

After we'd had our fill of the images, Martin put the book back on the shelf and said, "Don't forget to touch the Bible after, just to be on the safe side."

We both touched the Bible before leaving.

From then on we secretly consulted the book, at least once a week, hiding behind one of the shelves and ogling at the pictures.

* * *

Saint Saviours' was a comprehensive school, slap-bang in the middle of some of the roughest areas of Dundee: Fintry, Whitfield, Craigie and Douglas; so it had its fair share of psychos, hard men and general nutters. They had three main pastimes during the lunch break: playing a gambling game called pitchy, which involves throwing coins up against the wall, the winner being the one who gets his coin closest; smoking round the back of the boilers; and, of course, fighting and bullying. Martin and I came from the Ferry, one of the better areas of Dundee. We were bussed in to Saint Saviours', along with about forty to fifty other children, because it was the nearest Catholic School. Hence we were labelled 'snobs', 'toffs' or 'poofs' and were considered good bullying fare for the yobs during the breaks.

The library was a good place to escape to, to avoid getting beaten up, but the best place was the Chess Club, because we could eat our lunch there; and also because we liked playing chess, I suppose (we were both on the school chess team). It was run by Mr Fitzsimmons, a very amusing and charismatic chemistry teacher, but with a very short temper. He was well known for his angry fits, often reducing strapping lads, a foot taller than him, to blubbing wrecks just by screaming and shouting at them. He sometimes seemed as if he was about to have a nervous breakdown; eventually he did, but years later, once we'd all left the school. So while the Chess Club was a great place to hang out, it was wise to be on your best behaviour, since Fitzy – never call him that to his face – could drop in at any time to check up on you.

In the winter, when it was very cold, the classrooms got a bit chilly, even with the heaters turned on full. So Mr Fitzsimmons used to light up all the Bunsen burners on the workbenches, which were situated along three walls of the room, as well as the one on top of his desk, at the front. He left them on the slow, yellow flame and not the strong, ferocious, blue flame, but it was dangerous enough leaving unattended teenagers surrounded by flaming burners. It also created a rather mysterious atmosphere, like sitting in some pagan temple. I'm sure if some health and safety inspector had come along, he would have got rapped for it. But Fitzy was ever the rebel. This was 80s Britain, where teachers were striking and stopping all extra-curriculum activities in protest at Thatcher's budget cuts and pay rise refusals, and his Chess Club was the one remaining club in the school; all the others – sports, drama, photography, etc. – had been stopped after the first year. I think he supported the strikes, but he just loved chess. He had, after all, coached the famous Paul Motwani, a previous pupil at the school and huge chess star, who went on to become Scotland's first Grand Master.

So one Tuesday lunchtime, during our second year, in the

heart of the cold Scottish winter, we were sitting eating our lunch and playing chess in the chemistry lab / Chess Club, the Bunsen burners full ablaze and Martin said, "Watch this!" He went over to the workbench at the side of the class and moved his hand through the flame. "See, if you move your hand quite quickly through the flame, it doesn't burn."

We all have a fascination with fire. It must be human nature, part of our instincts, left over from prehistoric times where fire meant warmth, protection, hot food, story telling but perhaps also excitement: sex by the fireside? We've all set something on fire just for the fun of it: a candle, a firework, a match or a whole box of them all at once, thrilled by the little explosion, the sudden blaze. "Come on, guys, are you chicken?" Martin ribbed us.

We didn't need much persuasion, most of the boys and a few of the girls left their chess games and took turns putting their hands through the flame, feeling the slight warmth, but moving fast enough so as not to get burnt. I went to the burner on the teacher's desk, standing on a chair so I could reach it. Of course, just my luck, as I was putting my hand through the flame, Fitzsimmons came in, took in the scene – and went berserk!

"You, Beech! I can't believe it!" he shouted, already turning red.

Most people had backed away from the burners when he came in, but he'd caught me red-handed, seen me through the little window on the door before he even came in. "Can't I even leave you a few minutes, without you getting up to something?" he bellowed.

"Sorry, sir," I said meekly, looking down at my shoes.

"And here was me, just trying to be nice and warm the place up for you a bit." He looked around and caught Martin smirking. "I bet this was your idea wasn't it, Martin?"

"What? No, sir," he protested, but he wasn't fooling anyone.

"Right the pair of you, out! You're banned for the rest of the week."

There wasn't going to be any discussion, so we gathered up our things and made for the door. Fitzsimmons went around the class turning off all the burners. "Get back to your games the rest of you, and you can freeze for all I care!" He glared at us as we headed out the door.

"Nice one, Martin," I said accusatorily to my friend, who'd got me into deep water once again, or rather, thick ice in this case – it was one of the coldest days of winter, there was deep snow and thick sheets of ice everywhere.

The yobs were all having snowball fights and worse – pushing people to the ground and burying them with snow they kicked on top of them. Ron Knight, one of the chief psychos, spotted us, came along and shoved me to the ground and started kicking snow on me. "Sandy, you poof! Come and play snowballs instead of that poofy chess."

One of his mates, Grant Bishop grabbed some sand from a big bin of the stuff, officially used to help melt the ice, and threw some in my face. He also stuffed a handful down the back of my neck. "Hey, the Sandy Beech needs some more sand."

"You've just been checkmated by a Knight and a Bishop," joked Martin. He often used his humour in such cases, and by keeping the lowlifes amused managed to deflect most of their violence. While the pair of bullies guffawed, Martin grabbed me up off the ground. "Come on, Sandy." He led me away and once we were out of earshot he said, "Let's head to the library." He didn't want the others to know we were going there, since they'd just call us 'swats' and 'poofs' and probably pelt us with more snow and sand. We still had about forty-five minutes to kill before the end of the lunchtime break, so it seemed like a good idea.

The library was very quiet, just a few bookish types, perusing the shelves or sitting down reading at one of the desks. We blended in, although I was leaving a little trail of sand from the stuff Grant had put down my clothes. After aimlessly looking at a few books in the various sections, we found each other in the religious section, in front of the shelf with the infamous 'Witches and Warlocks'.

Martin took it off the shelf. "May as well have a gander," he said.

We looked through it, page by page; no matter how many times you looked at this bizarre tome, you were still spellbound, feeling a strange mixture of curiosity, horror and titillation as you took in the pictures – both drawings and photos. "Do you think those are actual devil worshippers, taking part in real black masses, or just models pretending?" asked Martin.

"Don't know. What, are you thinking of applying for a job as a model for the next edition?"

He laughed. "Who published this thing anyway?" He found the answer on one of the pages near the front. "Six-six-six publishing," he read aloud. "Geeze, the devil himself! Quick we'd better touch the Bible before we go." Lunchtime break was almost over.

"What do you think would happen if you touched it with the Bible?" he asked.

"Don't know. Probably nothing. Try it and see," I said flippantly.

"I'll hold this. You get the Bible." He was serious.

I rolled my eyes. "Okay, and then let's get out of here before the librarian wakes up and nabs us."

He held the volume of 'Witches and Warlocks', and I got the Bible, a big leather-bound edition, further along the shelf. It had probably been consecrated by the Bishop, the real Bishop that is, not Grant Bishop. I touched it onto the perverse, evil tome that Martin was holding and the pages burst into flames in his hands.

"Ahhh!" He started screaming. We both panicked. He dropped the flaming book to the floor, and I quickly placed the Bible – which had escaped unscathed – on top of the shelf, no time to put it back in its place. Then we both legged it out of the door.

Luckily, I don't think the librarian had seen us at all, engrossed as always in the latest potboiler she was reading. We ran downstairs and back into the playground, praying that we wouldn't be found out, or that we hadn't set the library on fire. There were no smoke alarms in those days, but I assumed the librarian wasn't that dozy that she couldn't react to the smell of smoke and douse a book with the nearest fire extinguisher.

* * *

The first class of the afternoon, Maths, went as usual, but halfway through the second class, English, there was a note passed round to all the teachers and everyone was convoked to the hall for an emergency assembly. When we got there the place was packed; all the teachers and pupils were present, as was the librarian, who for once looked emotional and agitated. Martin and I looked at each other uneasily. He put his index finger to his lips. Of course, I wasn't going to say anything. It was a golden, universal rule we'd learned since primary school; never grass, and especially never own up to anything if you know what's good for you.

Miss Gruffy, the assistant-head led the proceedings. She had a formidable presence, despite being only about five-foot-two. Greying hair cut short, icy-clear blue eyes which no one dared look into for more than an instant, built like a bus – not fat just solid, matriarchal, I suppose you might say. She'd been a missionary nun in Africa in the sixties and seventies, no doubt striking fear into the hearts of any cannibal tribes who dared defy her. She'd been awarded an MBE no less, before leaving the cloth and taking on a new mission: trying to keep us lot on the straight and narrow.

She held up the charred remains of 'Witches and Warlocks', holding it at the extreme corner between her thumb and forefinger, as if it was some filthy rag; I suppose it was in her eyes, both literally and figuratively. "Who's responsible for this?" she boomed, and then looked round the assembly hall, trying to detect any sign of someone who might know something. We all kept our eyes down and remained mute. She let us stew in silence for a good two minutes, before eventually saying, "Fine. No one's going to own up. The library's closed for the next two weeks."

She dramatically dropped the scorched volume into a wastepaper bin, which had obviously been put up on the stage beside her for this sole purpose. She looked out at us again and finally thundered, "God is not mocked!" Clutching the Bible – I'm sure it was the one I'd discarded previously up in the library, she glared at us for a few more instants, then strode furiously off the stage.

Chapter 2

The Call of the Bongos

Even after this episode, I still wasn't entirely convinced of the veracity of the supernatural, witchcraft, etc. I'd seen the pages go up in flames, but thought it might have been Martin who'd rigged the whole thing, lighting them with a hidden match or cigarette lighter. I confronted him about this just after the incident but he denied it. "Are you nuts?" he said. "Do you think I'd do that just for a joke? Plus, look at the state of my hands." There were several blisters on his fingers where the fire had burned him.

"So what, you're saying that it just spontaneously combusted?"

"Yes. That was one evil book."

* * *

With us being banned from the Chess Club and the library being closed, I thought the rest of that week would be hell. Stuck out in the cold, nowhere to hide from the hard-nuts; but it wasn't actually too bad. Apparently, word had got around that we were responsible for burning the book and almost setting the library on fire. Fortunately the librarian had reacted in time and used an extinguisher to douse the flames; a scorch-mark on the carpet remained and would serve as a reminder of this bizarre episode. The psychos regarded us with a new respect, if short-lived; in a couple of months they were back to picking on us as usual. I did, however, suffer some fallout. The day after the book burning, I was walking round the back of the boilers with Martin and a few other classmates – always a bit risky, but sometimes we went that way to go between classes, rather than walking the other way which took a lot longer. Some guy I didn't know and that I'd never even noticed before – he must have been two or three years above us – just came up to me and punched me right in the face, then wandered off without a word. We found out later that he was called Dougie Mitchel and that he'd been a big fan of the sordid tome we'd destroyed.

I'm sure Mr Fitzsimmons suspected we'd had something to do with the incident, but to his credit he never said anything. He welcomed us back to the Chess Club the following Monday, just issuing us with the warning, "Mess with fire and you'll get burnt. Mess with me and I'll have your livers on a plate." He was only half-joking. He was well known for being borderline. Sometimes he used to aim his car at pupils when he was driving into the car park and they had to jump out of the way.

* * *

So we toed the line. Ate our lunch and played chess. Went to classes. Stayed out of trouble, or tried to anyway. Often trouble came looking for you at Saint Saviour's, in the form of Rodney or Grant or Dougie or Mike or Wayne; all the thugs seemed to have names like this, as if their parents had perused a top ten of hardmen's first names in deciding what to call them at birth.

Being called Sandy Beech didn't help. Our family's little joke. I come from a long line of Sandy Beeches. The first-born son being called Sandy since as far back as anyone can remember. I almost escaped, since my dad was actually the second born and his parents wittily named him Sonny. But his big brother, Uncle Sandy, was a bit of a rebel and ran off and formed a rock band and changed his name to Stoney. He let it be known to all and sunder that no way was he going to be continuing on with this ridiculous tradition, if and when he decided to have children. So Dad – thanks a *lot!* – solved this problem simply by calling me, his firstborn son, Sandy.

What with the ribbing, the bullying, the difficulty of being taken seriously any time you phoned up and gave your name somewhere, you'd think someone, somewhere down the line would have shown a bit of mercy to his offspring, but no, our family were more of the mentality 'I've suffered and so will you.'

So the bullies had their fun with me whenever they got a chance; shoving me to the ground and sitting on top of me – 'I'm sitting on the Sandy Beech'; flicking sand or dirt or water at me, or even bits of fish from the canteen or local chipper; burying me in the long jump sandpit; or just chanting 'Sandy Beech, Sandy Beech, Sandy Beech' at me.

Thankfully, even the bullies matured a bit in third or fourth year, hormones started kicking in and they moved on to chasing girls. Their main interests now were snogging between smokes round the back of the boilers, slow dancing and more snogging at the regular school discos, holding hands, and dates after school. Some of the lads claimed to have lost their virginity as young as fourteen or fifteen.

* * *

I was a bit of a slow starter in this area. I'd held hands with a couple of girls, kissed them, been 'going with' them, as we said in Dundee, but nothing very serious. Going on a date was out of the question, since my parents were strictly against such antics until you were at least 18.

At one point though, I did get the serious hots for a girl, a crush which lasted all the way from fourth year to sixth year. Gabriella. She arrived at the beginning of fourth year and was in most of my classes. She was black and she was gorgeous. Her family had moved from Kenya when her dad had got a professor job at Dundee University. She was one of three siblings: her big brother Michael went into fifth year, and she and her twin brother Gabriel came with us into fourth year. Michael, Gabriel – her parents were obviously staunch Catholics, drawing on the names of the two archangels from the Bible. I suppose they couldn't exactly use the third archangel, Lucifer, to name their daughter, so lacking imagination they just called her Gabriella. There was something diabolical about her though, in the way she seduced many of the boys and probably a few male teachers in our school, with her exotic accent, her big, flirtatious brown eyes, her long eyelashes and her exquisite body – a perfect mix of slenderness and curvaceousness. She led us on with her lilting tones and provocative glances, only to refuse the advances of anyone who tried it on with her.

Dundee wasn't exactly cosmopolitan back then. There were a few Indian and Pakistani families living in the West End or in the Ferry, a few Chinese – the ubiquitous Chinese restaurant and Indian corner shop, but black people, whether African or Caribbean, were non-existent before their arrival. Our school had been 100 per cent white before they arrived. So to me – a pale-skinned, blonde-haired, blue-eyed boy – Gabriella's beauty seemed to be from another planet. I was smitten by her, but for fear of my mates' ridicule and a humiliating knockback, not to mention my inherent shyness, I kept my attraction to her secret. I allowed myself only the most furtive of looks; her long brown legs, sexily displayed in as tight a miniskirt as she could get away with, drove me especially wild.

One morning – it must have been halfway through fourth year – we were sitting in RE (Religious Education) class, and had been given some boring quiz to do by the teacher, Mrs Willis. She'd left us on our own, presumably to nip off for a fly smoke. Martin had a bright idea, as always.

"Hey, guys, we'll each write the name of the girl we fancy the most on a bit of paper, mix them up and then pull them out one by one and try to guess whose is whose."

And the point being? I felt like asking, but I didn't want to be a killjoy, so I duly wrote in block capitals – to avoid detection by my handwriting – GABRIELLA NDUGU. My 'mates,' who were grouped around the desk Martin and I were sitting at, all did the same. There was: Stewart Keillar, or StewK / Stookie as we nicknamed him, due to the fact that he seemed to spend half his life with a plaster 'stookie' on a broken arm, leg, wrist, etc. – due to bullying and falling off his bike or out of trees; Stephen Cummings, nicknamed Cum-boy – as he had a penchant for scuddy photos, or more cruelly Scum-boy; Alan Mashburn, nicknamed Mushy or Mushroom man; and of course the ring-leader, Martin Cardosi, nicknamed Dozy or Dozy bastard or Dwarf – as in Snow White and the Seven, even though he was above average height. My name was silly enough that it didn't really require any modification to produce a nickname, although sometimes people called me Beach-boy, or Sandyman; however the latter pissed off the biggest boy in our year, Gary Sandeman, so people tended to avoid that whenever he was around.

"Right, we ready?" enthused Martin. "I'll pick them out."

He picked out one of the scrunched up bits of paper and read out, "Marylyn Monroe. Okay very funny! Stew I suppose?" We all knew he had a thing about the American sex symbol, even though she was dead years before we were all born. Stewart just smirked.

"Next, Samantha Fox. Cum-boy, I presume?"

"This game is just stupid!" I blurted out. I was starting to have an uneasy feeling and made to grab for the three remaining bits of paper.

Martin got there faster. "No, no, come on, let's see." He opened the remaining bits and read out in a loud voice, so that half the class must have been able to hear: "Sabine, blank and ah-hah – Gabriella Ndugu!" He threw down the bits of paper to prove the veracity of what he'd just read out.

My reddening face removed any doubt as to who'd written the latter. Sabine was the sexy, blonde, French teaching, exchange student. *Everyone* fancied her, that was no secret. Alan must have written that, he hadn't even bothered with block capitals but just used his easily identifiable scroll. As for the blank piece, who else could it have been but Martin, the smart-ass initiator of the game.

I tried to protest. "It was just a joke. She's quite sexy, but I don't really fancy her!"

They all came back at me together. "Yeah right!" said Martin. "Bullshit!" spat Stewart. "You dog!" added Steve. Alan just burst out laughing.

Thankfully the teacher came back just at that moment. "Right, have you all finished the quiz? No? Come on, you've got five more minutes."

Everyone got back to work. Gabriella wasn't in my RE class, but word quickly got round, so that by the end of the day, she, and probably half the school knew about my (no longer secret) crush on her. She confirmed she was aware of my feelings by staring suggestively at me during our chemistry class that afternoon and winking at me as I went out the door at the end of the lesson. Would there be chemistry between us? Or would she just lead me on, like she'd already done with a few other poor saps, before crushing me with a humiliating knockback?

* * *

The next morning I had art lessons first thing after registration. Gabriella wasn't in the same classroom as me for this, but in the one next door; so quite often at the start of the class, I'd go out to the common area, shared between the whole art department, to choose articles from the big rack of stuff that could be used for still life drawings. That way I could see Gabriella, who usually did the same; we were both doing still lifes for the O-grade art exam. This time she was already there, rummaging through bits of driftwood. I went casually over beside her, avoiding eye contact but taking in her delicious perfume, and went to pick up a piece of driftwood. As I did so, she grabbed the other end of it, and a second piece of wood and started drumming a beat, while blowing into a few bottles that she'd positioned on the shelf, to produce a tune! I looked up and she just grinned and winked at me again.

My face reddening, I grabbed another piece of wood and a couple of other things – a sheep's skull and a green wine bottle, and just headed back to my class. Was she into me or just teasing me?

During the morning break, I recounted the incident to Martin and posed the question, "Do you think she might like me?"

"In your dreams, Sandy! She's just leading you on."

"So you don't think I should chat her up or try and ask her out?" Did I even have the guts to speak to her? Maybe Martin would boost my confidence; maybe pigs would fly.

"Yeah, go on. You may as well get your knock-back over with."

Great! Thanks a lot Martin, I thought sarcastically to myself. *You're a great help.*

"Don't even know what you seen in her. Can't you just fancy blondes with big tits like the rest of us?"

I'd never really thought about it that much. I'd always just preferred girls with dark hair and dark skin – few and far between in Scotland, especially back then in the eighties. When I first set eyes on Gabriella, my heart started beating like the bongo drums.

Prince, once famously said that the difference between white men and black men, was that white men hear opera singing when they are in the throes of lovemaking and black men hear the bongos of the jungle. He was forgetting about those white men like me with 'jungle fever;' and I suppose there must be black men afflicted with 'opera fever' who prefer white women and opera singing.

* * *

The school year ran its course. Gabriella flirted mercilessly with me, and my 'mates' and the usual yobs slagged me even more than before, but after a few weeks this treatment died down. Gabriella lost interest; either she figured out that I was too timid to make a move on her or maybe she thought I didn't fancy her that much after all. As for the rabble, they found other things to poke fun at; in my case they just went back to beating me up – physically and figuratively – about my name. Gabriella and I became friends, or at least close classmates, I suppose you could say. She was in quite a few of my lessons, so we ended up working together. I grew to like her not just for her looks but for her enthusiasm and intelligence. I was usually top in most subjects and she wasn't far behind.

"Well done!" or "Good work!" she would sometimes say to me when I got a particularly excellent mark in an exercise.

This made a nice change from the usual "Swat!" or "Bloody robot!" which others would often call me. There was an atmosphere of inverse snobbery at Saint Saviour's among a lot of the pupils, where it was cool to get low marks and where you were despised if you were intelligent, worked a bit and got good marks.

I was glad when fourth year ended. In Scotland you are allowed to leave school aged 16 and thankfully most of the psychos in my year took this option, moving on to technical college, apprenticeships, unskilled labour or prison in some cases; apparently Ron Knight ended up doing a couple of years for GBH – grievous bodily harm.

* * *

The final week of fourth year arrived with blazing hot temperatures, well, hot for Scotland anyway, 28°C or 82°F. The exams were over and those who'd already turned 16 and weren't continuing their education at the school had all left. Those of us remaining were all itching to get away. The smell of freshly cut grass wafted in through the open windows, filling us with longing to be outside, to be off for the adventures of the summer holidays. One strange event did occur that week that left us with something to brood over during the holidays.

Like every end of year, a big school mass had been planned for the last afternoon. Mr Roberts – the head of the music department – led the band, playing the hymns on the piano on such occasions. This band included the official brass band / orchestra, various rock bands, and basically anyone else who could play an instrument and whom he'd managed to rope into taking part. This included me since I could play the keyboards, although sometimes he made me play the xylophone. There was also a choir of about ten girls; no boy in his right mind would have joined as it would have been considered 'poofy.' A couple of days before the big send-off, he assembled us to practise in one of the big music rooms.

We all referred to Mr Roberts – but never to his face of course – as Rabbie, due to his love of Scotland's famous poet, Robert or 'Rabbie' Burns. He was always coming out with obscure quotes from Burns' poems. He also had an uncanny talent of always seeming to know what mischief we'd been up to, before anyone else and before it seemed possible that he or any of the teachers could have known. For example, one weekend Martin and I had been playing at climbing trees in the local park with another kid, Ignatius Sloss – who'd fallen and broken his leg; Stookie had been spared this time. Ignatius wasn't even in our school, but the very next morning, Rabbie bade Martin farewell from that morning's class saying, "Oh Martin! 'Wilt break thy neck ere thou go further.' Eh?"

Rabbie was a great musician, a virtuoso pianist, in our eyes. He took boring old hymns and jazzed them up, getting some of the rock band guys to do guitar and drum solos. He also used the piano as a means of communication, during the class or practise session, when quoting Burns failed, as it quite often did. Half the time we didn't know what the heck he was getting at. He'd play things on the piano: fairy music to ridicule the 'hard men' as they walked to the front of the class, funeral marches when someone got summoned to see the head or assistant-head, or ominous classical overtures when he was annoyed with someone. He had a tune for every occasion, and always played them brilliantly.

So, at this practise, one of the drummers, Mark Smith, turned up late. Mark was in fifth year, a bit of a psycho, but one of the few who'd stayed on past age sixteen. Rabbie looked at his watch and quipped "'Nae man can tether time or tide.' Eh, Mark?"

Mark just glared back at him and sat down at the drum kit. So Rabbie started playing the theme tune from the film 'The Omen' on the piano. Suddenly the crucifix, which had been hanging above the blackboard, fell down and the plaster figure of Jesus broke into several pieces on the floor! There was a stunned silence. Rabbie got up from the piano stool, walked over and picked up the little wooden pieces of plaster. He held them in his hand, looked down at them and then just flung them into the wastepaper bin beside the blackboard.

He went back to the piano, and as if the incident had never happened, said, "Right! Let's get back to the hymn: 'All Things Bright and Beautiful'".

* * *

But for that incident, all things would have been bright and beautiful that summer. Our family took us all off to the sandy beaches of Blackpool for the holidays and I would lie in the sun – plastered in sun cream, to protect my pale, white skin – dreaming of the silky black skin of Gabriella and fantasising about what it would be like to be with her. However, the scene of that crucifix falling down kept playing over and over in my head. I suppose it could just have been the vibrations from the music, but it seemed that some other power was at work here; something uneasy and supernatural – like the 'Witches and Warlocks' book which burst into flames.

We all pretend to be rational, logical, empirical thinking citizens of a modern world but bubbling below the surface lie our primeval fears, our pagan practises, our superstitions: beware of black cats that cross your path or of walking under a ladder, a broken mirror brings thirteen years bad luck, the rabbit's foot, the crossed fingers, the missing row 13 on public transport. Ever noticed – on planes, trains and buses – how the row numbers just jump from 12 to 14?

Chapter 3

The Devil Inside

Fifth year came along. Cool – no more yobs! Well only in the lower years, and you didn't have to deal with them much unless you were a prefect, and who in their right mind would sign up for that?

Miss Gruffy cornered me one day at the start of the school year, as I was making my way past her office on the way to a class. "I noticed you haven't volunteered to be a prefect. You know it's a privilege to carry out such duties. It gives you responsibility. Even employers can be impressed by the mention of it on your curriculum vitae."

"Well, I'm kind of busy with the Chess Club and stuff," I replied weakly. I didn't want to be policing the playgrounds and corridors during the breaks, no matter how good it looked on my CV.

"Nonsense!" she said raising her voice a bit. "You could do both. You only need to be on duty a couple of breaks every week. Come on, Sandy, you're not going to let me and the school down are you?" She stared expectantly at me with her icy blue eyes. I knew she was on the verge of giving me an angry reprimand if I refused.

"Well, okay then," I stupidly agreed.

"Great!" She smiled. "I'll add you to the list. Just check with Alice Peterson, for the rota."

Alice Peterson. Even better. She was a short, frumpy, do-gooder. Short black hair. Holier than thou, no nonsense attitude. In short a bit of a pain. As soon as she found out I was on the list she started badgering me.

"So can I put you and Jim Smith down for Thursday lunchtime?"

"Er, I've got something on that day. Special training session at the Chess Club. Can't really miss it. I'm on the first team and all that."

After about a week, I ran out of excuses. So I found myself one Wednesday lunchtime on corridor duty with Jim Smith. I didn't really like the guy. He was an average height freckly, curly, ginger-haired kid, who fancied himself as Bruce Lee just because he'd done a few karate belts. Still, at least he might be able to use his skills in defending us a bit if we got hassled by some yobs. Corridor duty meant patrolling all the school corridors, which were out of bounds to the lower years: the first to fourth years. You got the usual little tykes, and some not so little, trying it on: hassling you, name calling, even physical violence at times.

So that Wednesday, towards the end of the lunchtime break, we were patrolling the maths corridor – always a hot spot, since it was a great short cut taking you from one side of the school to the other in about 30 seconds, rather than the five minute walk if you went round the long way via the sports fields. Maths was on the ground floor, and there were two upper floors with parallel corridors – also usable for short cuts. On the first floor there was the Geography/History/Modern Studies department and on the second floor Languages.

We got to the west side of the maths corridor and caught three boys red-handed, walking through towards us from the other side: second years. I recognised Rodney Lear's younger brother, Shaun, just as much a psycho as his elder brother, who used to be in my year but who'd just left at the end of fourth year.

"Come on, lads," I said. "Get back the way you came. You know you're not allowed through here."

The just laughed and ran off back down the corridor to the east side.

"I'll check they don't try and go through Geo or Languages," said Jim. He walked quickly down the corridor.

"Okay." I waited on the stairway on the first floor exit:

Geography level. If they cut through Languages or Geography, they'd have to go past me: the second level had no other exit on this side, apart from this stairway. I couldn't just wait on the ground floor, because the first level also had a corridor at this side, leading off towards the English and Computer studies departments.

In a few seconds the three of them came running along the Geography corridor, with Jim in hot pursuit. "Stop them, Sandy!" he hollered.

"You lot, come on, that's enough! Shaun, mate, give it a break!"

The cheeky wee brats tried to get past me. I grabbed for Shaun, the other two managed to get past and down the stairs.

"Hey let go! I've got a class to go to!" He was squirming like a little snake, but calmed down as Jim grabbed him too.

I would have just let him go with a warning, but Jim insisted on taking him to see Gruffy. She gave him a big lecture:

"Prefects are just doing their jobs... you have to respect the rules of the school... we can't have people cutting through corridors just when they feel like it. You're on detention for the rest of the week, starting this evening, you and your two comrades in crime."

Jim had recognised the other two and given her their names; she would no doubt summon them later for a similar lecture.

"But Miss, we were just going to class," Shaun protested.

"No buts. Now off you go, before I add another week's detention."

Shaun's face reddened with anger, but he held his tongue.

"Well done boys," she said to Jim and me as we were leaving. Keep up the good work."

I cringed; this prefect malarkey just wasn't me.

When we were all out of earshot of Gruffy, Shaun muttered at me, "My brother's going to *get* you."

"What? You little creep... just leave him out of it!" I protested.

He just glowered at me and wandered off to his class.

* * *

The next day, during the morning break, Shaun brushed past me and said, "Rodney says you're claimed. After school tonight. Be there if you *dare*!"

"What? This is just stupid." I was about to try and reason with him, but he wandered off nonchalantly. You can't reason with psychos anyway.

Martin had been standing beside me and had heard. "Yikes! Rodney! You're as good as dead."

He was only half-joking. Rodney was about a foot taller than me. He'd always had the undisputed reputation of being the hardest psycho in our year. I had seen him in action when he'd sent a classmate to hospital back when we were in first year. Walloped him in the jaw with a hockey stick during a match and claimed it was an accident. The poor wee guy had his jaw broken and needed about twenty stitches. Not to mention numerous playground fights where he'd always demolished whoever he was up against. I was going to have to find a way out of this.

"Couldn't you fight him instead?" I pleaded to Jim – he was at least half responsible after all.

"Rodney Lear? Are you *mad*? If I were you I'd make myself scarce – bunk off the last period or something."

So much for being able to fight like Bruce Lee. Maybe I would just have to leave early and avoid the scrap altogether. I'd never played truant before – 'bunking off' as we called it, but this was an emergency. The problem was, how would I get home? I'd only brought enough money for the school bus and the service bus was a bit more expensive. Walking home would take ages; it was about five miles.

I decided to play sick half an hour before the end of the last class and then hide out until the school bus came. It usually arrived five or ten minutes before school finished; this would, hopefully, allow me to get on the bus before Lear showed up.

Last class that day was chemistry with Fitzy.

"Okay, Sandy, go and see the school nurse," said the Fitz, when I told him that I was feeling sick. "Or, come to think of it – just head off early and go rest at home."

I said thanks and hastily left. Good old Fitzy! My heart was thumping as I hid in some bushes, waiting for the bus to arrive.

The bus was thankfully a full ten minutes early and the driver let me on no problems. I stashed myself near the back of the upper deck and took furtive looks now and again out towards the school gates beside the bus stop. Still no sign of Rodney, even as the school bells rang to mark the end of the day. Maybe it had just been Shaun trying to get me to freak out.

The usual Ferry people got on. Martin came and sat beside me. "You Sand bunker!" he cried.

"Yeah, right. Any sign of Rodney?" I asked nervously.

"Nope."

Had it all been a big bluff from Shaun? Had I escaped unseen? The bus closed its door and set off. I started to relax. Then, after about five minutes journey, up the stairs came Rodney! He was accompanied by one of his hard-nut mates, Dylan McGrath, who'd also left after fourth year. They'd got on our bus and hidden downstairs!

"You leave my wee brother alone, ya bass!" he shouted, storming up the corridor towards me, his wide eyes boring into me demonically.

I was trapped! He pushed the people in the seat in front of me out of the way and started laying into me. I tried to fight back but only landed a feeble blow to his chin, while he managed to pummel my head with a good five or six sledge-hammer punches, before Martin and a few big sixth year boys managed to pull him away. My head was throbbing, my left eye and my lips already swelling up.

Martin did his best to console me, but I remained stunned for the rest of the fifteen-minute trip. When I got home I went to my room and let my tears of pain, of frustration, of hate, burst out.

* * *

My mum, once she'd coaxed the story out of me, gave me ice packs to sooth my swollen face. The next day she subtly applied some foundation powder to disguise my black eye and sent me packing, back to school. I may have taken a hiding, but I wouldn't let 'them' have the satisfaction of seeing how bad it had been.

I'd had it with prefecting though. For the next month or so, I came up with excuses every time Alice cornered me to try and pin prefect duty on me. Or if I did agree, I'd bottle out later, playing sick, or inventing some other reason for not being there. Then I just worked up the nerve and knocked on Gruffy's door.

"Yes, come in!" she shouted from within her lair.

"I can't do the prefect duty any more, miss. Too busy with my studies and other activities." I handed her back the prefect badge she'd given me when I'd signed up.

She just stared at me disgustedly for a few seconds, then eventually said, "Being a prefect is an honour and a privilege, you know."

She paused for a few more seconds, maybe waiting for some kind of rejoinder from me. I felt like saying, *Yeah, it's a real privilege to get your head panned in by the biggest hard man in the year,* but I just remained silent.

"Oh, get out of my sight!" she finally cried.

I quickly left, glad to be rid of that cursed prefect badge and back to keeping a low profile.

* * *

I studied hard in fifth and sixth year, staying top of the class in most subjects. I chose Physics, Chemistry, Maths, English and French as 'Highers' in fifth year; then just Maths, Physics and

Chemistry at sixth year studies level. I got excellent exam results and decided to apply for a degree in Electronic Engineering. Anyone that was good at maths got pushed into engineering by the career advisers at our school. That was where the jobs were, and well paid jobs at that. I got accepted by several universities, but decided on Strathclyde, in Glasgow.

I was tempted to stay in Dundee, especially when I found out Gabriella would be studying medicine at Dundee University. But that would have meant staying at home and I was too keen to flee the nest, to fly with my own wings, to have some freedom.

A final night out was organised, at the end of the summer, by one of the more popular girls in our year, Jennifer Ross. She'd managed to hire a trendy place called Sinatra's: a restaurant / bar, with DJ and dance floor, in the centre of town, for quite a reasonable price per head. Everyone in our year was invited, plus, eventually, girlfriends or boyfriends. Even a few of the cooler teachers got an invite. So it was quite a big turnout that Saturday night, the last week in June of 1988. I was particularly excited – maybe this would be my big chance to finally get something going with Gabriella. I had nothing to lose anyway – school was over and we were all going our separate ways.

We all got dolled up in our swanky clothes. Most of us were eighteen or about to turn eighteen. In a lot of pubs you'd be asked for ID and a strict policy was applied of alcohol for eighteen-year-olds and over only; they would even turf you out if you were under age. However, for this night, our little private function, a blind eye would be turned: even us seventeen-year-olds would be served, no questions asked. This suited me as I would turn eighteen only later in July.

I caught the bus with Mushy and Dosy who lived near my house.

"Nice tie, Sandy!" said Martin. I was wearing one of those thin piano ties that were all the rage back then. This was the height of the ska movement and we were all heavily into groups like Madness, Bad manners and the Specials.

"Cool brogues, mate! You must've spent ages shining those; you can almost see your face in them!" I returned the compliment.

As for Mushy, he had the regimental stay press trousers on and had made an effort to look smart, sporting a tie with a saxophone on it, but with his gangly figure and beaky nose, well he wouldn't have looked cool in anything. All in all though, we were smartly turned out.

When we saw the girls, or should I say young women, we were all stunned. They were all perfumed and made-up, wearing elegant, low-cut evening dresses.

"Hey, check out your femme fatale!" said Martin, discreetly indicating Gabriella. He didn't have to, I'd noticed her as soon as I walked into the function suite. She was wearing a sexy red mini-dress and her hair was done up in a frizzy-bob style. She looked more beautiful than ever. All the girls did, but she outshone them all in my eyes.

There was some food, in the form of a help yourself buffet – sandwiches, hot dogs and the like, but this party was more about sex and drugs and rock 'n roll, or rather, by order: alcohol, the demon drink – Scotland's drug of choice, to help us lose our inhibitions; loud disco music – a mixture of ska, rock and pop, to get us mingling and in the mood for love; and sex if you were lucky, or more likely a late night kebab or pizza to finish off the night.

I made the mistake of trying to match Cum-boy downing whisky and lemonades. He was obviously used to copious drinking and I wasn't. I had never drunk more than a glass of wine or a couple of beers. So after about five of these my head was spinning. I even had to lie down on the bench seating at one point, but Martin and Mushy dragged me up and off to the toilets to splash water on my face.

"Come on, you twat, the night's still young," said Martin.

"Drink some cold water."

"Yeah, you need to get up on the dance floor and score with one of the chicks," Alan chipped in.

I still felt a bit rough when we got back, so I switched to cokes and fresh orange and lemonade for the rest of the night, much to the amusement of hardened boozer, Cummings. "You total poof!" was his remark.

Halfway through the evening, I eventually plucked up courage and asked Gabriella for a dance.

"Sure, Sandy! Like the tie by the way!"

I wasn't sure whether she was taking the mick; her eyes had that usual teasing, playful look.

She was a great dancer and seemed to be enjoying herself. We stayed up for a few dances and then I invited her for a drink. "What's yer poison, darling?" I put on a silly cockney accent.

"Ooh, what do you propose, big boy?" she replied, ever the flirt.

"I'm going for a fresh orange and lemonade." I didn't want to end up like Stevie Cummings who was now staggering round the dance floor, leering at the girls and making obnoxious comments.

"Okay, very wise. Make that two. I've been on the white wine, but I think I've had enough too."

We sat at the bar and I held her hand. She didn't resist – that was a good sign.

"So off to Strathclyde, Sandy, I'll miss you. I'm staying here in Dundee."

"Never knew you cared."

"I do care. I like you, Sandy."

She was sincere! All this time! I could have been with her long before now.

She went on, "Okay, you were a bit of a tube when I first met you back in fourth year, but you've matured. We all have I suppose." Ah! Just as well I did wait till this moment.

At the end of the evening the DJ played a slow number: fittingly "Lady in red" by Chris de Burgh.

I danced with Gabriella and held her close. The rest of my mates had paired up with girls too: Martin with Alice Peterson, the head prefect – no accounting for taste; Alan with a cute blonde called Claire Evans; even Stevie had made it with Jennifer Ross. Jennifer liked her booze too apparently. I tried not to imagine what raunchiness they'd get up to later. The boys 'discreetly' gave me thumbs up or all okay gestures from across the dance floor.

At the end of the dance we kissed, long and sensuous. I felt euphoric, like I was floating, touching the ceiling almost.

People started saying their goodbyes, leaving as couples or small groups; sex or a consolation kebab beckoned. I couldn't take her home with me, since my parents would go berserk. I wasn't even eighteen and they were strictly 'no sex before marriage.'

"So, your place or mine?" I used the cliché jokingly, but desperately hoping that 'her place' was up for grabs.

"Er, my parents are in."

"Hmm, yeah, mine too actually."

"I've got a plan though, if you're up for it. My cousin's a student and he's left me the key to his digs. He's away to Glasgow for the weekend. We could go there if you like?"

My heart began beating faster. This was finally happening. "Okay. Cool!"

We walked hand in hand to the nearby university residence where her cousin stayed, chatting a little and stopping a lot to kiss. I could hear the bongos trying to keep up with the rapid beat of my heart.

Her cousin's room was decorated with African masks, wooden sculptures and lots of strange necklaces hung all over the walls but I wasn't really interested in the decor. We were all over each other as soon as we got in the door, caressing each other, taking off each other's clothes. I took in her perfume, felt her smooth, soft, black skin and submersed myself in the ecstasy of that first night of lovemaking.

We had sex three times and I could have continued all night, but she reminded me that our parents would give us hell if we didn't get home soon, so we shared a taxi back at around four a.m. – her house was on the way back to mine.

"Good night, Gabriella! Let's meet up soon." I kissed her goodbye, as she got out of the taxi.

"Night, Sandy!"

* * *

The first few weeks of those summer holidays were just bliss. We both had part-time summer jobs. Her's was an admin job in a factory; mine was doing household items delivery. This thankfully left us with loads of time together. We'd go for romantic walks by the river Tay, sit in cafés, looking into each other's eyes, and make use of her cousin's room for rapturous bouts of sex.

Unfortunately though, about halfway through the summer, our love affair was brought to an abrupt end. We'd been having delicious morning sex in Gabriella's cousin's room and it was almost lunch time.

"Fancy a pizza, Sandy? My treat." She proposed.

"Okay. Sounds like a plan."

"You just stay here and relax. I'll nip out and get them." She was already getting dressed.

"Sure, thanks, Gabriella."

I lay back, still naked under the sheets, with that feeling of deep relaxation and contentedness you get just after sex. She'd only been gone about five minutes when I heard a key turning in the lock. Surely that couldn't be her already? Had she forgotten her money or something?

I sat up in bed. A young black man came in, and on seeing me, shouted, "Hey! Who the hell are you?"

I presumed, correctly it turned out, that this must be her cousin, Isaiah. He was supposed to be away working on a student placement in Edinburgh all summer, but had come back for some reason.

"I'm Sandy. It's okay; I'm a friend of Gabriella's."

This didn't seem to calm him down. He took in the scene, me lying naked under the sheets, the smell of Gabriella's perfume, a used condom still lying knotted on the bedside table...

He muttered something I didn't understand – presumably in Swahili, then asked, "Where is she, the little whore?"

"Don't call her that. She's my girlfriend."

"Okay, *lover* boy, just get dressed, you're leaving."

He at least had the decency to turn his back while I quickly got dressed. If I could just get away before Gabriella got back, I might be able to intercept her. Damn, one of my shoes was missing! I hunted around for several minutes and found the shoe, which had ended up under a pile of magazines. Isaiah just stood there the whole time with his arms folded, glaring at me. I was just putting on my shoes when there was a sound at the door. Oh no! It was Gabriella returning with the pizzas!

She came in and said, "Got your favourite, Sandy, tuna and sweet corn!" before she had time to see that we were not alone.

"You little tramp!" shouted Isaiah. "I left the backup keys for this place with your parents. How the hell did you get your hands on them? Anyway, just wait till they hear about *this!*"

"What! You don't have to tell them! Just leave them out of it!" she pleaded. Then she broke down crying.

I went over to console her, but Isaiah grabbed me by the wrist and started pulling me towards the door. I tried to resist but the guy had a powerful grip. At the door I struggled even more and he grabbed my hair, pulling it so hard that a lock of it came away in his hand. He eventually managed to throw me out into the corridor, then stood in the doorway shaking something at me – it looked like one of the strange necklace things that had been adorning his walls.

"Headcase!" I shouted and tried to shove past him to get back inside, to Gabriella.

She came up behind him. "Just go, Sandy! It's all right. We'll see each other later. I'm sorry."

I reluctantly left. To top it all, I'm sure that bastard cousin must have eaten my pizza when I was gone. And what did he pull some of my hair out for?

I hoped things would blow over after a few days, and that we'd get back to going out together, but when I called her house there was either no answer or one of her parents replied and told me to stop calling, that Gabriella was busy and didn't want to see me.

About a week after the incident, I fell violently ill. I vomited up anything solid I ate and so was reduced to soups, juice and tea. At night, I had terrible nightmares; a perfectly smooth, spinning sphere would appear, but when I looked closer it became more and more coarse, lumpy... until I got really close and saw it for the churning, dirty mass of organic material that it was. I would look closer and closer and it would become more and more rough, squirming and filthy... and I was sure I could hear the noise of the beads on the strange necklace that Isaiah had shaken at me.

The doctors carried out various tests, but didn't find anything. Had Isaiah somehow poisoned me? I looked up some books on African customs and practises; apparently their witches or sorcerers use peoples' hair to put an evil spell on them. The use of gris-gris beads was also common to invoke or to ward off evil spirits. Was I the victim of some curse from the evil Isaiah?

When the date to start university arrived, I summoned up all my energy, packed my bags and headed off to my new residence in Glasgow. I'd lost about a stone in weight by this time. Fortunately, the move away from Dundee (and from the source of the spell?) seemed to do me good and I started to eat solid food and gradually got back my strength.

It seemed that I'd just had my first encounter with African witchcraft. Unfortunately it would not be my last.

Part II

Chapter 4

The Ghost of Gabriella

I made new friends at university, did well on the various modules of my course and took part in the extracurricular activities that Strathclyde had to offer: sport (I joined the hockey team and used the gym and pool) and partying. I 'settled in,' I supposed you could say, but the rupture with Gabriella weighed heavily upon me. I could somehow still feel her presence: her gentle touch, the sweet exquisiteness of her perfume, her warm smile and of course her alluring body. I ached with longing to be with her.

I continued to try to contact her by telephone but the snubs by her parents eventually discouraged me and I tried a different tactic: letter writing. This was in the days before internet, email and mobile phones. I managed to obtain her address by phoning Jennifer Ross, then wrote her about six letters during my first month at university, but with no reply. It was her home address in Dundee – she was still staying with her parents, and I suspected that they weren't giving her the letters.

I thought about going back to Dundee for a weekend or even skiving off university on a weekday and trying to track her down. Maybe I could find her at the medical faculty in Dundee? But I was still wary of the poisonous Isaiah; I didn't want a repeat of my illness, which I was sure he had caused. So I came up with the idea of sending a letter to Jennifer and getting her to pass it on to Gabriella – to her alone, and as discretely as possible. I wrote:

Dear Gabriella,

I'm missing you so much. I can't stop thinking about you. Are you okay? I hope you didn't get into too much trouble after your cousin, Isaiah, busted us during the summer.

How are your medical studies going at Dundee University?

Please call and let me know how you are doing or reply by letter [I gave her the address of my halls of residence and the telephone number of the phone in the hallway – someone would usually answer it and come and get you or leave you a message if you were out].

I'm doing okay. My course is interesting and Glasgow is cool. It would be great if you could come and visit – maybe some weekend?

Love you forever,
Sandy

Jennifer assured me that she'd passed on the letter and a few days later I received Gabriella's reply by post:

Dear Sandy,

I miss you and I love you too. But our relationship is impossible. I ask you please – just forget about me and get on with your life.

I don't want you to go through any more pain. My family are dead set against us. Since they found out, I'm not allowed out, except to go to classes and labs. My parents and Isaiah are watching me like hawks. They will not hesitate to take measures against you, if they find out we've been seeing each other.

My father has informed me that I will return to Kenya and work as a doctor there as soon as I have completed my degree. He says I will marry a good Catholic Kenyan man only and already has some 'respectable suitors' apparently.

Forget me Sandy.

Please just enjoy your life.

Yours,
Gabriella

* * *

So that was it. Our brief relationship was over. I didn't try to get in contact with her again, but my obsession with her remained. I would spray myself with the same perfume she used, and close my eyes and imagine she was there beside me. The little photo she'd given me of herself remained in my wallet, and I'd look at it endlessly; and I'd play the music we'd danced to over and over again in my room, until the guy next door would hammer on the walls and shout, "Switch that off, Sandy, you sad git!"

I hoped desperately that she might change her mind, dreamed about receiving a call from her, or a letter saying that she was coming to see me, her family be damned. But that never happened.

I eventually confided in my new best mate, a curly-headed business studies student called Gregor Evans.

"I just can't seem to get Gabriella out of my system."

"What, some bird? There are lots more fish in the sea! Come on, mate, you can easily find some new filly to get down with," he replied, mixing his animal metaphors.

"I don't want a bird, or a fish, or a young female horse!" I moaned. "I just want my African goddess back."

"Yeah, well, from what you've told me, she doesn't want you back. Plus it seems that her cousin's ready to practise his voodoo magic on you again. Time for a quick exit if you ask me!"

"Tell you what," he continued. "Why don't we go to the Todd on Saturday night? Last time I was there it was crawling with cute, female, nursing students from the infirmary. There were even a few darkies, if that's really what you're into."

This was the Lord Todd student bar, which was run by Strathclyde, but open to all. It was frequented mostly by Strathclyde students from the surrounding residences on the campus, but also by working men from the adjoining neighbourhoods and students from other colleges / universities, including –

according to Gregor – nurses from the nearby Royal Infirmary. The place was a lot mellower than the huge students' union in John Street; the music wasn't too loud, so you could actually have a chat with your mates. Our residence was about two minutes walk away, so the place was like our local.

"Okay," I agreed. "Just don't call black people *darkies*. They'll likely do their voodoo on you; or simpler, just punch you in the face."

"Okay, Mister Politically Correct. Whatever you say."

* * *

Saturday night arrived. Gregor was 'champing at the bit,' to use one of his animal metaphor clichés. He came to my room at around six p.m. "Right! Are we on?"

"What already? I think I'll make myself a bite to eat first, before we go out."

"Nah, screw that! Let's just get fish suppers and a bottle of thunderbird to wash it down."

Gregor was nothing, if not refined. Thunderbird is a cheap fortified wine. We used it as a warm-up for a night of binge drinking or rather he did and usually roped me into drinking some of the sickly stuff.

That night our group consisted of me, Gregor, John Mingus, a tall, dark-haired student of Scottish History and champion of the nationalist cause, Nick Stevens, a wispy blonde-haired, English 'settler' who'd moved from London to Aberdeen with his parents when he was six, conserving his grating English accent, and even more annoyingly, who supported the Tories (why he hung out with us was a bit of a mystery) and Ian Shanks, Gregor's pal from school, a die-hard goth with long, straight, brown hair, who was studying some kind of arts degree at Stirling. Shanksy, as everyone called him, often came and stayed with us for the weekend, crashing in Gregor's room or sometimes mine. I was impressed with his ability to sleep the whole night, sitting fully clothed in a chair.

We got our fish suppers at the local chipper, three bottles of Thunderbird and a couple of six-packs of beer at the 'offie' (off-licence), then all went back to my room, where we ate, drank and played cards till around eight-thirty p.m. Then we headed out to the Lord Todd bar.

"How d'ya feel, Sandy? Buzzing? Ready to get into those sexy nurses?" prompted Gregor.

"Yeah, whatever," I replied. My head was 'buzzing' a bit though, the strong wine and beer taking effect.

The pub was busy, standing room only. We all went up to the bar area and Gregor ordered the first round of drinks. 'Heavy' beers – pints – for all of us. "Six o'clock. Check it out," he whispered at me.

"What? It's eight-thirty-five," I said looking at my watch.

"No, you idiot. Behind you. It's the nurses!"

I looked round as discretely as I could, there were a group of five girls and two men, all clutching their drinks and chatting away. One of the girls was Pakistani or Indian and one was black; the 'darkies' Gregor had been referring to.

"Let me break the ice," said Gregor, ever the ladies man. Although on this occasion he started by going over and talking first to the two male nurses; he'd already made their acquaintance apparently on a similar night out at the Todd. After a few minutes the rest of our 'gang' sidled over and Gregor made the introductions, to the two guys and the five women.

"I'm Sandy! Pleased to meet you," I said to the black nurse. She was shorter and rounder than Gabriella, her skin lighter, her face less attractive. Nevertheless I found her quite sexy; her eyes reminded me of Gabriella; she also seemed to be wearing the same perfume.

"Janet MacDonald. How's it goin'?" Her accent was pure Glaswegian.

"Janet MacDonald, eh. Doesn't sound very African! Where you from?"

"Glasgow born and bred, would you believe? My dad's Scottish; Mum's from the Caribbean."

"Ah, Bounty, the taste of paradise!" was the only thing I could think of saying. I noticed Gregor, who was listening in, rolling his eyes at me. Janet laughed though, showing off her beautiful white teeth. After a few drinks, even the lamest of humour seems funny.

"What about you?" she enquired. "You don't sound like a local."

"I'm from Dundee."

"Ah! Nobody's perfect!"

People from Glasgow and Edinburgh think it's amusing to do down my hometown. "Cheeky!" I played along with her mickey taking.

Gabriella had been perfect in my eyes. Irreplaceable. But here I was, already trying to replace her; going for another girl who mildly resembled her.

We stayed in the Todd pub until closing time – one a.m., then the nurses invited us all back to their digs at the 'GRI' (Glasgow Royal Infirmary). They took us through the main entrance, up some stairs to the third floor, then along some corridors to their common room.

One of the male nurses, John Tavish – he seemed to be the ringleader or at least the biggest party animal – offered round a bottle of whisky. Despite feeling the effects of all the alcohol we'd consumed I accepted a small nip, just for show; I was glad when one of the girls, Gladys Gaynor – GG as they called her, proposed us cups of tea a bit later.

"Tea! Ya wimps!" Gregor chided me and some of the others who took up the offer, he was still knocking back whiskies with the two Johns.

Around three a.m. the girls headed off. None of us had

'concluded.' It seems I'd come the closest though with Janet.

"I think she likes you, mate!" teased John Tavish.

"Yeah, you're in there, pal," said Chris McGurthy, his nursing student mate.

"Yeah, she's cute," I said, playing it cool. "Maybe I'll ask her out or something next time."

"Never mind *next* time," said Tavish. "She's begging for it. Go and chap on her door now! It's room three-o-six, just down the corridor on yer right there."

Egged on by Tavish and the rest of the lads, I strode off down the corridor, found room 306 and knocked.

"Who is it?" Janet's voice came from within.

"Sandy!"

"Oh." There was a pause; maybe she was reflecting on whether to let me in or tell me to get lost. "Come in then for a bit, if you like."

I went in and shut the door. She was sitting up in her bed, dressed in a white night-dress.

"So, d'you have a good night, Janet?" I went over and sat on the bed beside her.

"Yes, not bad, a good laugh. Bit tired now though."

Was that a subtle hint?

"Yes, know how you feel. You're only young once though, eh?" I put my arm around her shoulder and went in for a kiss. She didn't resist. We necked for a few minutes. I went to caress her breasts which I could see bulging under her semi-transparent nightie, but she pulled back a little.

"Maybe we should just call it a night, Sandy," she said eyeing me with a somewhat wary look.

"Okay." I kissed her one last time, full and long. Closing my eyes, smelling her perfume, imagining she was Gabriella.

She broke off, and said, a little more insistently, "I think you should leave now, Sandy, don't you?"

"Okay. I'm really into you, you know. See you at the Todd,

next week?"

"Okay. See you."

Feeling rather frustrated and rejected, I left. Instead of heading back to the common area where the lads would probably still be hanging around, I headed on further down the corridor where Janet's room was, not really thinking where I was going.

After taking a few turns, left and right, walking down various corridors, I suddenly realised I was completely disorientated. Where was the way out? How could I get there without going back via the lads and their jeers? I was still on the third floor and the exit was on the ground floor; maybe I could get back down there via another staircase and then find my way to the same doors we'd used to enter the hospital complex. I noticed that at the end of most of the corridors, there were signs indicating different hospital departments with arrows pointing the way: Neurology, ENT, Oncology, etc. and sometimes there was an arrow pointing to the nearest exit; there were also green fire-escape signs in most of the corridors, lit up, showing the way. I followed these and came to a different stairway, went down three flights, and came to a door, but there was a big red placard on it which said, 'This exit should be used in an emergency only; alarm will go off on opening.' Just great! I didn't want to set off the alarm in the middle of the night, wake up the whole hospital and have some security guard chasing after me.

Apart from this fire-escape, there was only one other corridor leading off; the sign just said 'General Surgery,' but the corridor was pitch black – a fuse must have blown or something. There was no way I was going down there to stumble around in the dark looking for another escape route.

I went back up the stairs to the first floor. The signs pointed down one corridor to Cardiology and another to Canteen, Severe Burns Unit and Maternity. I took the latter, figuring the canteen would likely be close to the main exit.

I arrived at a branch pointing Canteen, Maternity one way; Severe Burns Unit the other. I was about to continue on the corridor towards the canteen and maternity, but a strange noise coming from up the other corridor made me stop for an instant. What was that? A kind of tapping? No, more like the shaking of beads. It reminded me eerily of Isaiah shaking his creepy gris-gris at me.

I gave myself a shake. *Ignore it, Sandy; just stick to the plan and head towards the canteen.* I was about to obey my thoughts when I heard, "Sandy!"

Someone had just called my name from somewhere inside the Severe Burns Unit. Had I imagined it?

"Sandy!"

There it was again! Someone was definitely calling me. But who? What was this? Had the lads followed me and were they playing some kind of prank to try and scare me? I wouldn't put it past them.

I walked warily up the Severe Burns corridor and located the door where the noise seemed to be coming from. *Severe Burns,* I thought to myself, *Rabbie would feel right at home here.* I gave a little laugh, trying to reassure myself. But thinking of Rabbie, his icy stare, and the episode with the crucifix, had the opposite effect. I nervously swallowed my saliva and opened the door.

It was the ward, apparently, for people who'd suffered severe burns. In the dim light I could make out ten beds, all occupied with heavily bandaged patients. They all appeared to be asleep. But then I heard the tapping beads noise and a hoarse voice called out again.

"Sandy!"

It came from the bed in the far corner of the room. I made my way over past the other patients – silent but for the sounds of their laboured breathing and the soft beeping of various monitors and equipment. The patient calling me was propped up at an angle in the bed; the sheets covered her up to the waist, but the visible upper body was completely covered in bandages. I presumed it was a woman, judging by the voice and the slight bulge of her breasts under the bandages. I sourced where the tapping noise was coming from: she clutched beads – rosary beads perhaps? – in her bandaged right hand, and was hitting them against the intravenous drip by her bed.

"Sandy! Forget her. Just forget her!" she rasped.

"What? Forget who?" She made me so uneasy I could feel myself shaking. "And who are you anyway?" I tried to steady myself. I just wanted to get out of this place as soon as possible.

"It's me! Sister Bernadette! But please, Sandy, listen! You need to listen! Forget Gabriella, forget African women, and avoid them at all costs. I know you're attracted to them, but you're in grave danger. *Please!* You have to… I'll pray for you…" Her voice trailed off. I could hear how she toiled just to breath. She was extenuated, but she continued tapping the beads, as she tried to get her breathing under control to be able to continue.

"Hey. Take it easy. Maybe I should call a nurse or something." I didn't want to do this, because how could I explain my presence here; but I didn't want some nun dying on me either.

"Don't worry about me," she whispered, as if reading my thoughts. "My time on this earth is almost over. They got to us with fire. The whole convent. Up in flames. All the others dead… and soon I'll join them. A few more hours, maybe days… and then may God accept my soul." She paused again, murmuring prayers while she clutched the beads.

When she seemed to have stopped praying, I asked, "Who's *they*?"

"The witches, African devil worshippers, Gabriella and her lot," she went on. "You have to avoid them. Try and control your *lusts!*" The word 'lusts' obviously disgusted her.

She was freaking me out. How did she know about me and Gabriella? I was about to try and question her further when one of the monitors of another patient began beeping loudly and a red light started flashing above his bed. I went over and saw that the heart monitor showed zero heart activity – he was flatlining. Damn, what was I going to do? Should I make some attempt at heart massage? Surely, someone on the night-staff would be along in a couple of minutes; then how would I explain what I'd been doing here?

Bernadette read my mind again. "He's already dead. There's nothing you can do. Most of us are terminal in here."

"How can you be sure?" I asked, but I knew she was probably right. All the patients in the room were covered in bandages like Bernadette; their chances of recovery must have been slim. I could hear voices and footsteps from down the corridor, from where I'd arrived. Damn! I had to leave. Was there another way out of this ward?

Bernadette tapped with her beads and pointed her hand towards another door to the side of her bed. Her powers of telepathy were uncanny! As I went out, she hissed a final warning.

"Forget Gabriella. Don't go looking for her and don't try to replace her with another black woman! I'll pray for your safety!"

I shut the door just as I heard the main door to the ward opening and what must have been the medical team bursting in. I was out in a nondescript corridor. In one direction it led off to more wards, but it could well have been a dead end. The other direction led back round past the door the medics had just come in. I headed stealthily down that way. Thankfully they'd shut the door behind them and I assumed they must have been busy trying to revive the patient who'd flatlined. Or were simply verifying his death? Anyway, I didn't hang around to find out. I walked quickly down the corridor marked Canteen, Maternity.

The canteen was empty and in darkness and I continued on. At last, a sign marked Exit! I was just about to follow this, but I glanced towards the entrance to Maternity and noticed something strange on the floor. *Oh my God!* There was blood seeping out from under the door! What the hell was going on? This was the stuff of nightmares. I went closer to the Maternity Ward and from within came the noise of a baby crying; but not just crying, this was a blood-curdling shrieking, louder and more horrifying than any scream I'd ever heard – from baby, child or adult. Nauseous with apprehension I wrenched open the door, expecting to be greeted by some gruesome scene, but when I entered suddenly everything went quiet. The blood had disappeared and all I could see were the peacefully sleeping mothers and their newly-born infants.

Was I going mad? I had to get away from the hospital! I sped off towards the exit sign, and followed the signs down a flight of stairs to the ground level and the main doors. I got out at last, and breathed in huge lungfuls of the cool night air.

I ran back the short distance to Murray Hall. The place was deathly silent; everyone had gone to bed, even the night owls like Nick. I locked myself into my room and tried to get to sleep but my head was throbbing, and not just from the effects of the alcohol. I could hear the nun's warnings and that terrible shriek, playing over and over in my head.

Chapter 5

The Thirteenth Nun

What had really gone on in the hospital that night? Had I imagined the whole thing: the bandaged nun and the shrieking baby? I kept it all to myself anyway; when Gregor or some of my other university mates enquired about what happened with Janet, I remained vague: "Oh, we just kissed and stuff."

"And *stuff*. Yeah, I get the picture," was Gregor's rejoinder.

I decided during the week that I would go the following weekend, to see if I could visit the nun again, but during official visiting hours and in daylight. However on Thursday evening, I was having a flick through the local newspaper, which was delivered daily to our halls, and I noticed an article entitled, 'Sole Surviving Little Sister Succumbs to Wounds after Royston Fire.' I read it several times. Sister Bernadette did exist, or had existed rather – she'd died on Wednesday. There'd been a fire at the nearby convent in Royston a couple of weeks ago and all twelve nuns of the 'Little Sisters of the Poor' order had perished. Bernadette had been the twelfth – the last survivor. No suspicious circumstances according to the paper.

So, Saturday afternoon, I decided that I'd wander up to the convent, or what was left of it after the terrible fire. I looked on the map of Glasgow I'd bought. It was within walking distance of Murray Hall, up on top of a big hill beside three huge multis (high-rise flats). I set off just after lunch; I wanted to be back home well before nightfall. It wasn't raining thankfully – a bit of a rarity for Glasgow – but the cold wind made up for it. By the time I was over the pedestrian walkway, which crossed the motorway running alongside Royston, I could hardly feel my fingers.

The three multis loomed ominously; one was all boarded up

and uninhabited, except perhaps by a few squatters and junkies. The whole housing scheme was deserted, eerily silent. I turned left after the multis and on towards the convent, hugging the big wall on my left to shelter as much as possible from the wind.

When I was almost at the entrance to the convent grounds, a group of five boys approached me, crossing the street from the other side. They'd emerged from the houses behind the multis, most of which were boarded up, vandalised or both. They must have only been between the ages of ten and twelve, but I felt fearful and quickened my pace.

"Hey, big man! Going someplace?" jibed the tallest one, a freckle-faced, crew-cut sporting lad dressed in a tracksuit. He and his four mates blocked my path.

"All right, lads. How's it goin'?" I tried to play it cool and started to walk around them.

One of the smaller ones stuck out his foot and I stumbled onto the road, but managed to keep upright. They all laughed and another one of them spat on my jacket. I just ignored this and carried on walking, but they persisted. The tall freckly one shoved me in the back and shouted, "Think you're hard or something?"

I felt like laying right into him, but knew I wouldn't stand a chance: five against one, even if they were all a lot smaller than me. Damn! I should have got Gregor or big John to accompany me. But then I would have had to try and explain why I wanted to visit a burnt out convent.

"Look, lads, cool eh, I'm no' looking for trouble!" I tried to reason with them.

"Yeah, well trouble's looking for you!" One of them said, taking a swing at me, but I ducked and his fist hit the wall behind me.

"Ah!" he screamed, "Ya' total bas!" He stood rubbing his fist.

I'm sure he was about to give me a wasting with the help of his four sidekicks. Thankfully, just at that moment, a man wielding a baseball bat emerged from the convent gates and shouted, "Hey, you wee neds! Piss off and leave him alone!"

The gang all ran off, back towards the dilapidated houses. "Next time you're dead pal!" Freckle-face yelled a final threat at me from the opposite side of the street, before disappearing down the hill with the rest of them. Hopefully there wouldn't be a next time. This was the last time I was wandering up here by myself.

"Thanks for that," I said to the man who'd just saved my skin. He was in his forties, tall, with a gaunt face, bald on top, but with dark hair on the back and sides.

"No problem, my friend," he replied. "Some right wee psychos around here."

"D'you work at the convent?" I asked, noticing he was dressed in a janitor's overalls.

"Yeah, I do. I'm the caretaker. Although I don't know for how much longer. All the nuns just died in a tragic fire. I suppose you must've seen it on the news or in the papers."

"Hmm, yeah. I knew Sister Bernadette."

"Ah, poor woman. At least the rest of them died in the fire or soon after. She agonised in that hospital for two weeks before finally passing away. I visited her with my wife and son there several times; her burns were horrendous! We couldn't even talk to her, poor thing, she was in a coma. "

I was about to say, *That's strange, she was wide awake when I saw her,* but thought the better of it and just nodded grimly.

"Why don't you come in for a cuppa tea? I was just about to have one," he offered.

"Sure."

"I'm Dave, by the way."

"Sandy. Good to meet you."

He had his own little family house within the convent grounds. He showed me the burnt out remains of the main convent building on the walk to his house. "The place is gutted. I doubt they're going to rebuild it. Looks like I may be out of a job soon."

He showed me in to the living room of his little house and went off to make the tea in the kitchen. I had a gander at the photos on the mantelpiece. There was one of him and what I presumed to be his wife and son. There was also a group photo of the nuns. I counted – a row of seven standing, with six sitting in a row in front – thirteen of them.

He came in and found me looking at it. "That was taken just a few months ago. Can't believe they're all dead now. Well, all except Gabriella, she pissed off back to the Ivory Coast, just a few days before the fire."

Gabriella! I almost choked on my tea, which I'd begun sipping. I recovered quickly. Common enough name after all. "That her there?" I pointed to the only black nun – she was standing at the top left of the photo.

"Yeah, just beside Sister Bernadette."

I saw that Bernadette was a rather young nun, quite attractive, even dressed in the staid habit they were all wearing. Gabriella was young looking too, she had a certain allure, nothing compared to my Gabriella of course. All the other nuns must have been over sixty.

"Those two got on great. Until..." he hesitated, looked at me, deciding whether he should give me the whole story.

I gave him my best sympathetic listener look.

"Well, until that skanky little whore, Gabriella showed her true colours and seduced my son. They were sleeping together on the fly, would you believe it! God knows for how long – Gabriella was here three years. Anyway, Sister Bernadette finally found out their little *secret* and reported it to the Mother Superior, Sister Martha. Gabriella was given a choice, repent and mend her ways or leave the order. Guess what she chose?"

"She left? Rather suspicious timing, eh, just before the fire," I remarked.

"Apparently she was already back in the Ivory Coast. Anyway, the police have ruled out foul play. A forgotten candle or cigarette was the cause, they say. Most of them smoked you know, one of their few pleasures in life."

"That your son, there?" I pointed at the other photo I'd noticed.

"Yeah, that's him, Andy. Would you believe the stupid little twerp's just taken off this morning? Caught a flight to Abidjan to go and look for Gabriella. He's only twenty. My wife and I are really worried."

Andy, Gabriella… suddenly I realised the nun in the hospital might have taken me for Andy, Dave's son. With her rasping voice, muffled by the bandages, had she actually been saying Andy and not Sandy? My head began to fill with doubts and conflicting thoughts. What if the nun had really been addressing this Andy guy and not me at all? But she knew about my attraction to black women. Or did she? Maybe Andy had the same 'affliction' as me, maybe even worse than me, since he'd jumped on a plane to the Ivory Coast in search of his Gabriella. And what about the blood I thought I saw, the shrieking baby? Just a shadow, a baby having a bad dream? Had the nun been raving nonsense about witches and devil-worshippers, and them having caused the fire? With all she'd been through, it could only be expected that she'd half lost her mind.

I even started to think about my story, with my Gabriella. Had I really been the victim of some curse from her cousin? What were those beads that he'd waved at me? Black magic gris-gris or perhaps they were in fact rosary beads like the nun? Thinking about it now, it seemed more likely they were rosary beads; her family were all devout Catholics after all. There was no curse, I tried to convince myself. I was just suffering from some stomach bug, aggravated by lovesickness. Nevertheless, I decided that I'd at least follow the nun's advice, whether it was meant for me or Andy; just forget Gabriella and avoid black women in general.

My tea had gone cold.

"I'd better be off. Thanks for the tea. Good luck with the job and everything. And I hope your son comes back soon."

"Thanks. I'll walk you down to the motorway flyover," he offered. "Make sure you don't get hassled by those neds again."

"Okay. Thanks."

On the way to the footbridge he asked, "So will we see you at Bernadette's funeral on Monday?"

"Euh, where is it? And what time?" I had classes and labs all day Monday.

"Funeral mass at 10 a.m. in Saint Mungo's followed by the burial in the Necropolis."

The Necropolis. It sounded like the title of some horror film. I didn't really fancy it. I'd have to miss classes and people at the funeral might delve a bit more into who I was and how I knew Bernadette. I felt guilty though about Andy; maybe if she'd actually spoken to him instead of me, he wouldn't have gone off on some mad lovesick quest to the Ivory Coast. "I'll try to make it," I found myself saying.

At the bridge, we shook hands.

"See you on Monday, then?" The pain was evident in his eyes, at losing Bernadette and the rest of the nuns, and on the disappearance of his son.

"See you there, yeah." Looked like I'd committed to going.

* * *

The rest of the weekend was rather subdued. Gregor and a few others proposed the Todd or the Union on Saturday night, but I said I wasn't feeling well. I used the same excuse on Monday morning when Callum MacKenzie, a guy on my course also staying in Murray Hall, who I usually walked in with, tapped on my door at eight fifteen a.m. I'd get photocopies from him later of that morning's classes and make it in for the labs in the afternoon.

Once he'd gone, I got on a pair of black stay press, a white shirt, my piano tie and a dark coat. I managed to put the tie on backwards, so that it just looked like a thin black tie. I didn't actually own a suit at that time, so this would have to do.

True to form, Glasgow offered up a cloudy, drizzly day. I'd been there two months and couldn't remember seeing the sun once. Saint Mungo's was just a ten-minute walk from the halls. I'd been there a few times for mass on a Sunday, but found the place rather cold, sinister even. Maybe that was just an excuse for not going more regularly. In truth, going to church, a Catholic school, grace before meals and so on had always been something imposed by my parents. With the new found freedoms of university and influences of new friends, I found myself rebelling against Catholicism: that I suppose, and just sheer laziness.

But today I felt a renewed fervour. I was going to pray for Bernadette's soul and the souls of her departed sisters of the cloth. I felt connected to her; even if her advice was probably meant for someone else, it applied to me. I may also have been the last person to talk to her before her death.

The funeral mass took a long time. Like in most deaths of a priest or nun, it was concelebrated by numerous priests, and there were long eulogies and special prayers and hymns. The huge crucifix which loomed over the altar was marked with the Passionists' motto: 'We preach Christ crucified.' I felt this really applied to Bernadette; she'd suffered horrific burns on what must have been at least ninety per cent of her body, and while her fellow nuns had been granted quick deaths, she'd agonised for two weeks in that lonely hospital ward before finally passing away.

* * *

After the mass, I met Dave and his wife Shona outside the church. They offered to give me a lift to the cemetery and I gladly accepted. While there was still only a light drizzle, the sky was getting darker and darker. The short drive to the burial grounds passed mostly in silence.

Shona did speak a few fitting words though about Bernadette. "She was a lovely woman, a fervent believer... She really helped the poor, as did all those in her order... An example for us all... We'll really miss her... May she rest in peace."

Dave and I limited ourselves to 'yeses' and 'amens.' I was a bit curious as to whether or not they'd heard from their son, but decided that this wasn't really the occasion to pry into such matters.

We arrived at the Necropolis, a sprawling burial ground with graves dating back to the early 1800s, although somehow it seemed more ancient, the looming weathered tombstones were like prehistoric monoliths. The ever-darkening sky added to the ominous atmosphere. As the priests said the final prayers for the soul of Bernadette, it was almost as dark as night. Then after the coffin with her remains had been lowered into the grave and a few of her close relatives and friends were scattering earth on top, the sun suddenly appeared through the clouds, shining brightly on the grave. It seemed miraculous; there were audible gasps; a few women broke down crying; even the priests seemed moved.

Dave and Shona asked if I wanted to come back for the collation which was taking place at the church hall. I thought about it, but decided against it; I didn't really feel like talking about how I 'knew' Bernadette, plus I had just about enough time to make it back for the first lab of the afternoon, if I left right then. I said my goodbyes and was just about to head off, when the Saint Mungo's priest, who'd been leading the mass and the graveside prayers came over and shook my hand. "Thank you for coming. God loved her and has taken her to be with him. May she rest in peace."

"Amen. Thank you, father." I nodded and made to leave.

"I've seen you in church a few times. I'm father O'Brien – quite often do the Sunday evening mass."

This was the one us students went to, if we went at all. It was at six p.m. on Sunday, allowing us time to recover from our hangovers. "Good you could make it. Did you know Bernadette well?" He gazed at me intensely.

Great! I thought. *An inquisitive priest.* "Just a bit. Recently. I visited her in hospital." I didn't want to lie to a priest. "Sorry I can't make it back to the hall. Have to get back to uni."

"Okay, son. God bless you. What's your name anyway?"

"Sandy."

"Ah, Sandy, eh? I think this might be for you. It was by her bed when she died." He handed me a folded bit of paper with 'Sandy' written on it in shaky handwriting; inside were the nun's rosary beads.

I felt the blood draining from my face. I clutched the paper and the rosary beads, managed a "Thank you father," then walked off in the direction of university. The sun disappeared as suddenly as it had arrived, and the darkness enveloped me.

Chapter 6

Frogs and Snails and Puppy Dog Tails

With such portentous signs, I endeavoured to knuckle back down to being a good Catholic boy; saying my prayers, going to mass – even if it was the post-hangover, Sunday evening edition with father O'Brien, and trying to control my 'lusts'. I didn't go chasing after women, especially not black women, contenting myself with the odd drunken snog. Towards the end of first year, I almost caved in when a persistent little blonde girl I'd been dancing and snogging with at the Union came back with me to my room.

We fondled each other on top of my bed, and I was aroused enough, even though she wasn't really my type: busty, white, blonde, not dark, slender and exotic.

"Fiona, it's been a good night, eh? I'm totally knackered though. Think I've had one drink too many," I reasoned with her. She was still clothed but lying on top of me.

"Come on, Sandy. Don't you want it?"

First year was almost over. Exams had gone well. The summer holidays were just a week away. Why not go out with a bang?

Control your lusts! I thought of Bernadette's warnings. Was that really what was holding me back, or wasn't it actually my stupid obsession with Gabriella, with black women?

I pretended to fall asleep, but I'm sure she wasn't fooled.

"Come *on!*" She shook me with all her force.

When I didn't respond, she angrily shouted, "You're so *weird!*" Then she left, slamming the door on her way out.

* * *

Second year was much the same as first year. I stayed in the same halls, but all my mates – Gregor, John, and Nick – moved into flats. It seemed it was the cool thing to do. It seemed I wasn't that cool. I still saw them a bit, but I was a bit miffed that none of them had asked me to be their flat mate. John's flat was a bit far from the centre, so he sometimes came and slept on my floor at weekends, when he'd missed the last bus and didn't want to fork out for a taxi. As did Shanksy. He was more Gregor's mate, but now that Gregor's flat was a bit far from campus, my floor or rather my chair was a better bet for sleeping over in Glasgow at the weekend.

I did have a couple of 'girlfriends' during the year. The first one was called Belén Dos Reis; she was a Spanish Erasmus student, studying history at Strathclyde for the academic year. I liked her warm smile, her big, brown eyes and her sexy, Spanish accent. I met her in the Todd one night, we chatted, she seemed nice and so I asked her out for a drink, one-to-one, the following weekend. I soon found out that she was really only interested in a platonic relationship. She confessed that she had a boyfriend back home and that she was saving herself for him. I stupidly persisted in going out with her for about three months – the whole of the first term, hoping she'd change her mind and allow her Latin libido to overcome her loyalty to her boyfriend; that she'd eventually give in to my advances, but she always pushed me away.

"Come on, Sand*eee*! I have a boyfriend already!"

On the last night before the Christmas holidays, I pulled out all the stops, taking her to a nice restaurant, with refined food, wine in posh glasses and fancy waiters. After the meal and a drink in one of Glasgow's more trendy bars, I walked her home. We stopped at the entrance to her halls of residence and I grabbed her by the waist. She'd never asked me in so far, but I was hoping that at last she'd surrender and invite me to her room.

"Belén, I really like you. You just turn me on *so* much." I looked longingly into her eyes, and moved in for a kiss.

We kissed for a few seconds, I could feel her hesitating, would her resolve, her fidelity finally cave in?

She broke off the kiss, looked me in the eyes and said, "I like you too, Sand*ee*, but we're just friends."

I'm sure Bernadette would have been proud of her; of me – not so much.

When I didn't release my grip around her waist, she shoved me away. "See you after the holidays."

Not if I saw her first. I couldn't believe I'd wasted so much time chasing after her. "Bye, Belén."

After the holidays I didn't bother going to see her again. We passed each other on the campus a few times during the rest of the year and just exchanged a quick "Hi," or a "Como estas?" And that was it.

* * *

Then there was Leman Dilovan. A Kurdish girl from Paris whom I'd met in the library, the first week of the second trimester. She had light brown skin and beautiful white teeth. I especially loved her teeth. Funny how we get hooked on little things: the darkness of someone's skin, the colour of her hair, the shape of her body, the smell of her perfume, the sound of her voice, the whiteness of her teeth. We pretend love is more about personality, how well we get along, the connecting of souls. Physical attraction, though important, is relegated to a secondary role. We're afraid to admit that deep down it's all about animal attraction: the look, the smell, the taste, the touch, the sound… and those mysterious pheromones.

I made the mistake of telling the 'lads' about my new lady friend, Leman, the Kurd. Leman. Kurd. They needled me endlessly.

"Have you squeezed Leman yet?" joked John. "I bet she was

like lemon curd when you were finished with her."

"How's Leman. She yer main squeeze now?" was Shanksy's attempt.

One Friday evening, Nick came by.

"Mind if I crash on your floor tonight, Sandy?" he asked. "Go on be a mate. Our year has a big do on tonight. It'll go on late and I can't afford a taxi back."

The cheek of the guy! I hadn't seen him since first year and he had the nerve to just drop in and expect to take up what little floor space was left in my room. I already had John and Shanksy staying over; they were already lazing around my room when he came by. This was just getting too much.

"Oh yeah," he continued. "Heard about you and the Leman. Have you squeezed yourself inside her yet?"

What a sleazeball!

They all started laughing.

"Well, since you mentioned it, I've got a hot date with her tonight," I said. "But it's too much of a *squash* in here, for me to bring back Leman or anyone else. How about giving us a break guys, and finding somewhere else to spend the night?"

"Yeah, maybe we should, guys," quipped John. "Wouldn't want to come back here and find Leman Kurd on the Sandy Beech."

I reddened with embarrassment and anger as they all guffawed.

The message had gotten through though. John said he could kip over on someone else's floor and persuaded the others to go and sleep over at Gregor's – it wasn't in the centre but was walkable.

It was true I did have a date with Leman, but I doubted she'd come back to my room. I'd been seeing her for a month and she was turning out to be a bit like Belén: nice-looking, sexy voice, liked going out, but *totally frigid* – well with me anyway. Still I wasn't giving up yet. We were going to a house party tonight; one of my hockey team pals, Dan, had invited me – it was at one of his friends' houses in the west end of Glasgow. Dan had given me the address. All you had to do was turn up, BYOB – bring your own booze; and as usual with these kind of student parties, you could bring your girlfriend, your friends, whoever you liked really, as long as they had booze too. The more the merrier.

She'd invited me to her student flat for a bite to eat, so I went there at around seven p.m. She shared with three other foreign female students: a French blonde called Sabine, a dark-haired Italian called Paula and a brown-haired German called Hilda. Like most Erasmus students they were always partying and were extremely popular with boys. They were all quite good looking, especially Paula, but I think the added attraction was simply that they were foreign – the little differences: hairstyles, clothes, accents and faltering English – just drove the men wild. Hilda and Paula were already out when I arrived. Sabine was just heading out with her boyfriend, Guillaume – also French.

Leman looked stunning that night, her smile more dazzling than ever.

"How are you, Leman? You look great! And what's that delicious smell?"

"Ah, a surprise! I made you a few Kurdish and French special-ities. Look some dolma – vine leaves stuffed with rice; tapsi – spicy peppers, aubergines, courgettes, and potatoes and here we have snails cooked in garlic and even some frogs' legs. Take a seat, tuck in." She poured us some good French red wine, none of your Buckfast or Thunderbird crap – typical sophisticated French.

"Looks good! Never tried frogs or snails." The snails actually made me feel a bit queasy. "Suppose there's a first time for every-thing. Thanks, Leman, you've really put in a lot of work to make all this!"

"Well I cheated a bit. Got the snails and frogs' legs from a French Deli."

"Didn't even know they existed in Glasgow. You'll have to take me sometime."

"Here squeeze some lemon on the dolma if you like."

"I'd rather squeeze you, my little Leman!" I shamelessly used the lads humour on her.

"Ha, ha! Never heard that one before." She blushed a little.

"This is really delicious, Leman." Even the snails were okay, chewy but mostly they just tasted of garlic. "Change from the usual student fare of toasties, pizzas and fish suppers."

We took our time eating and drinking, finished off her wine, then set off for the party in the west end at around nine p.m and caught a bus from Hope Street.

She brought another bottle of nice French wine; back then any normal wine tasted great compared to the El Dorado or Thunderbird we lads drank. As for me, I'd gone to the offie that afternoon. I was going to just get the usual: a six-pack of heavy and a half-bottle of cheap whisky, but I decided to go for the heavy and a full bottle of the whisky – it was only a couple of quid extra and there were two of us after all; I knew Leman wouldn't bring much.

The party was the usual student affair. Loud music, people sitting or standing around chatting, drinking, smoking. Food was limited to a few bowls of nuts and crisps. People just turned up whenever, invited or not, didn't really matter as long as you had your plastic bag of booze. There were a few guys from my hockey team, so I chatted with them a bit. I introduced them to Leman.

"French, eh, very swish!"

"Ah, Sandy, you lucky dog!"

"Good man, Sandy!"

In amongst the comments were the usual jokes about squeezing Leman. One guy came up with, "She seems like a nice girl. Kurd you please take it easy on her, Sandy." Everyone thought we were an 'item.' I was hoping that night would seal it.

At last, around midnight, she let me kiss her as we sat on the settee. Her lips were soft, her breath sweet from the wine. I savoured the moment, high on alcohol and love.

By two a.m. all our booze was gone. Leman had tried a few glasses of whisky, after much persuasion from me and some of the other partygoers – "Go on, it's Scotland's national drink." I'd offered some to a couple of hockey team mates; the rest – maybe half a bottle – I'd drunk myself. My head was spinning a bit. I could see by Leman's eyes she was half-cut as well, the drunkest I'd ever seen her.

"Come on, beautiful, let's get some fresh air and grab a taxi home."

It was a short walk to the Great Western Road; we held hands and necked on the way. Once there we quickly managed to flag down a taxi, no problems. Well, no problems flagging one down, the problems came later.

I gave the driver the address of my residence. Leman didn't protest. It looked like I was 'in there' as the lads would say. In the back of the black cab we embraced ever more passionately and began caressing each other. I could see that the driver was ogling us in the mirror. He made a turn into Killermont street and was passing the Anderston bus station when some drunken student stumbled onto the road, right in front of the taxi. Unable to swerve right – there was an oncoming bus, the driver braked and swerved left, up onto the pavement. There was a loud thump before the cab came to a standstill, more on the pavement than on the road. What had he hit?

I untangled myself from Leman and got out of the car to take a look. The driver was still sitting there stunned. The guy who'd caused the accident had legged it. There was a grey-bearded homeless guy shouting, "Look what you've done, ye eedjet!" He was struggling to hold back a big, black dog, which was howling and tugging at the leash. Beneath the car's back wheels were the remains of three puppies, their heads and bodies had been totally pulverised. The tails of one of the puppies was still quivering, in the throes of death. I swayed in nausea, held onto the back of the taxi and spewed my guts. The remains of undigested snails, frogs' legs, not to mention copious amounts of wine, beer and whisky, splashed all over the back end of the car, mixing in with the blood of those poor puppy dogs.

The driver was suddenly out of the cab. "Bloody drunken students! Look at the state of ma' cab!" he shouted, taking in the splatters of blood and vomit on his otherwise shiny cab.

"Never mind yer cab. Ye've killed my three pups, ya bastard!" screamed the homeless guy. "Few inches closer and it would've been me and Meg here." The dog, evidently the mother of the three pups was straining at the leash, growling and bearing her teeth at the driver.

Leman came over and tried to console the poor old tramp. "So sorry, sir!"

"No your fault, love. This psycho driver's the wan! I'm gonnae' get the polis onto ye'," he threatened the driver.

"Sod this!" The driver jumped back into his car and sped off, not even asking for the fare. Just too much hassle, even for a Saturday night in Glasgow? Or maybe he'd been having a fly drink on the job and didn't want the police coming along to breathalyse him. The sight of the crushed dogs and the puke made me gag and I almost vomited again, but held it in.

I pressed the fiver I was going to pay the taxi with into his hand. "Sorry for your troubles."

"Irreplaceable, those pups," he said. "At least I've still got Meg." Then he broke down crying. The dog, Meg, whimpered at his side.

We took him inside the station and I got him a cup of tea from the machine, while Leman sat him down on a bench. She then spent a good half hour consoling him and calming him down. I tried to offer a few compassionate words but mostly just stood there, uncomfortable at his weeping. For Jim, as we found out he was called, it was almost as if his own babies had been killed.

We dissuaded him from calling the police; no one had clocked the licence plate and, knowing the police, they wouldn't have been very sympathetic towards two drunken students and some smelly old homeless guy. After he'd calmed down, we said our farewells and then walked the rest of the way back to the campus, about fifteen minutes, mostly in silence. There was no more kissing. I tried to take her hand but she pulled it away. The night, so full of promise, was ruined.

* * *

When I went to see Leman the next day at her flat, she wouldn't even invite me in.

"I feel awful," she said. "My head hurts so bad. Why d'you make me drink that whisky?" She looked at me accusingly. It was about two p.m. and she was still dressed in her nightie. She did look pretty rough.

I couldn't remember forcing her to drink the whisky or the wine. It wouldn't have helped my case though to point this out.

"Sorry, Leman. Next time just stick to wine, eh?"

"There's not going to be a next time."

"Come on, Leman, it's just a hangover. You'll get over it." Apparently she'd never had a hangover, at least not one like this. "Why don't I nip down to the shop and bring you some Irn Bru?"

"Why don't you just get lost?" She slammed the door on me.

* * *

Leman never forgave me for that night. For the next couple of weeks I tried calling her and knocking on the door at the flat, but she was always 'out' – according to her flatmates anyway. I'd become persona non grata.

Two weeks later I was out with Gregor and Shanksy – it was a Saturday night, but we'd decided just to have a quiet drink at a pub called the 'Drum and Monkey.' I saw through the pub window, Leman walking arm in arm with Dan, my 'friend' from the hockey club.

"Don't believe, it!" I shouted angrily. "That Leman has already hooked up with someone else – one of my so-called mates!"

I was about to storm out and confront them, but Gregor held me back. "Forget her, Sandy! Isnae' worth it. Lots more fish, lots more fish."

Maybe it was time for me to try fishing in a different sea.

That quiet drink turned into a massive session. You drink to lower your inhibitions, to be with girls; and once they've left you, you drink to drown your sorrows.

* * *

I was starting to get sick of the whole scene: the mundane campus, the unattainable women, the inane parties, the macho drinking, the spewing and the hangovers. Halfway through second year, when they asked for volunteers from our course to go on Erasmus in France for the whole of third year, I jumped at the chance. My grades were good – still at or near the top in all subjects, and I could speak French, having done Higher at school and some optional courses at University; so they readily accepted my application. I was over the moon!

Five guys got selected to go to Nancy, two to Nice and two of us to Paris: me and an English guy from Hull, called Bruce. We all extolled the merits of this foreign exchange trip: international experience, improving language skills, making new friends and contacts, getting ahead in the job market and so on, but deep down the number one reason we were all going was for the sexy French women! I was especially excited about Paris, since it was very cosmopolitan – there wouldn't just be French, but women of all origins and colours.

The foreign Erasmus student girls were much sought after

here by us local lads, and I suppose the foreign male students were sought after by local girls – not that I paid much attention to that; but I was sure this rule would work for us in France, since we would be the foreign, exotic ones over there.

* * *

So for the rest of second year, I just concentrated on my studies. I toned down the partying and the drinking and avoided women altogether. Well avoided them in the romantic sense; I did of course hang out with girls in my classes and labs, at the halls of residence, and so on, but just as friends.

On the final Friday night before term, all the lads met up for a few beers in the Todd: Gregor, Shanksy, John, Nick, plus some of their other mates and I'd brought along some pals from Murray Hall.

"Take it easy with the French birds, Sandy, they're a dirty lot!" John joked.

"I'll try. It'll be tough!" I replied.

"Yeah, he'll be too busy with all those hot African women," said Gregor. "Paris is crawling with them."

Suddenly, I noticed an older guy sitting at the bar – it was Dave, the convent janitor. I'd never seen him in here before. I went over for a chat.

"Hi, Dave. Remember me? Sandy. How are you?"

"Oh yeah, Sandy," he said, recognising me. "So, so. Still in a job at least. They're keeping me on to supervise the site while it's demolished. Should take a year at least."

He didn't look that great. His face was even more drawn than the last time I saw him. "How's the wife? And what about your son, any news?"

"Wife's fine, holding up as well as could be expected. That Andy, he's driving us daft. He's become totally obsessed with tracking down Gabriella." He looked down at his beer dejectedly.

"What, you mean he still hasn't found her!" I exclaimed. "How long has that been, over a year-and-a-half?"

"He's been out there three times, would you believe? Goes for three months, the maximum stay on a tourist visa, then comes back and works to save money for the next trip, then heads off again, and so on."

"Hasn't mentioned anything about witches, black magic, that sort of stuff?"

He looked up at me sharply as if I was mad. "The only thing he's been bewitched by is that dirty whore's fanny!" he shouted.

A few people at the bar turned and stared at us, and the barman came up and said, "Oy, guys! Keep it cool, eh."

"Nae worries, pal," replied Dave. "I'm about to head off anyway. Too many of the idle unwashed in here for my likin'."

"No offence, Sandy," he added for my benefit. "You're okay, but a lot of students are total layabouts." He downed his beer and got up to leave.

"Sure I can't get you another?" I asked.

"Nah, maybe next time."

"Well actually I'm off to France next year. So I won't be around here for at least a year."

"Geeze, another one flying the coup. What is it wi' ye' young-sters. Scotland no good enough for yous'? Can yous' no' just settle doon' wi' a nice Scottish lass?"

No, if ye've got Jungle Fever like me and yer lad Andy, I felt like saying, but I didn't want to get him even more riled up so I just said, "Hope to see you when I get back, Dave."

"Bye, Sandy," he replied. There was a certain sadness in his eyes; he was no doubt thinking about his son. "Take care. Come back in one piece." Then he was off, and I got back to my mates.

The rest of the night was uneventful, but for the goodbyes. The lads all had their 'witty' send-offs.

"Don't forget to write!"

"Easy on the vino!"

"Don't turn into a frog!"

"Use a condom!"

I'd shaken hands with everyone and was about to head back to the halls with a couple of other Murray Hall pals, when a girl from my course, Lizzie Dunbar, came up out of the blue and kissed me on the cheek, saying, "Have a good time in France. Look forward to seeing you again in fourth year." Her hands softly touched my forearms, for an instant.

"Thanks, Lizzie. Look forward to seeing you, too." I gazed into her deep blue eyes for a moment, and then she just looked away shyly and left with some of her friends.

I'd always just thought of Lizzie as a classmate / friend. We got along great, worked together in a lot of labs, tutorials and so on, but she wasn't really my 'type.' She had pale, white skin, long blonde hair and blue eyes. The way she'd just touched me, though, her kind sincere words and the look in her eyes made me see her in a different light. Even her kiss; no kiss on the cheek had ever been as sensual.

I suddenly felt doubts about going to France, about leaving all my uni friends for a year, and even deep down about what was really my 'type'. Here was some beautiful blonde girl who seemed into me. Why hadn't I even noticed her for the past two years? Why did I obsess over coloured women, especially black Africans? Was this all just some stupid lingering sentiment from Gabriella and the fact that she was my first love? And hadn't that just been some adolescent, lustful fling that I'd stupidly become fixated on reproducing. Why didn't I just stay in Glasgow, get it on with Lizzie... 'settle doon' wi' a nice Scottish lass' as Dave had proposed?

Lying in bed that night, back in my room, I heard the nun's warnings in my head, *Forget Gabriella, forget African women, avoid them at all costs. I know you're attracted to them, but you're in grave danger... African devil worshippers, Gabriella and her lot... Try and control your lusts!* Surely just the mad ravings of some poor disturbed, indoctrinated, sexually frustrated woman. Maybe she'd even been jealous of Andy and Gabriella, the disgraced, young, African sister, sent back to her home country. What about the fact that she seemed to know me, about me, that she'd left me the rosary beads? Maybe in her confused state, she'd just got Andy's name mixed up and thought he was called Sandy.

I got up, switched the light on, took the beads out of my case where I'd packed them. They were meant for *me*, I just knew it, felt it in my guts. I looked at them, fingering some of the beads before coming to the little crucifix. It made me think back to the scene of the crucifix falling off the wall in Rabbie's band practice. Some of the choir had also been present at that practise. Including Gabriella, who had a beautiful voice. Everyone had been shocked when the thing fell down, but thinking back, I'd glanced at Gabriella and noticed that somehow she didn't seem as shocked as the rest of us. There had been an almost imperceptible little smile on her face.

Bernadette had probably wanted me to use the rosary to pray. To pray for what? Protection? Protection from what? From my lusts? From evil, African witches?

I switched the light off, held the beads and prayed a decade.

France was an adventure, I *had* to go. I couldn't cancel now anyway, everything was organised and booked. I'd take the beads with me to France. I'd be okay.

Part III

Chapter 7

The Erasmus Experience

For all my resolutions about toning down on the drinking, the partying and the womanising, I couldn't go to France on an Erasmus exchange for a year and not partake in the extracurricular activities.

Bruce was raring to go. "You know what France is known for?" he said on the flight over from Glasgow. "The three W's: wine, women and weed. This year's going to be awesome. Party time!"

"Weed? That's more Amsterdam, Netherlands, isn't it?" I retorted. I'd never tried the stuff, even though there had been a bit of it around in parties in Glasgow.

"France, too, mate, you'll see. They get it from the Netherlands, sure, but also directly from Morocco."

* * *

Turns out he was right. That very night we were invited to a party in our residence and they passed round a bong. I experienced the mellowing effects of weed for the first time. There were ten of us there, sitting around on chairs, the bed or the floor.

"Good shit, eh brother?" said Henry, an African American.

"Yeah, thanks for inviting us, guys." I nodded to Jonathan – he was the organiser, and we were in his room. He was a tall, blonde-haired English guy.

"You're welcome," he replied. You boys are gonna love it here. Parties galore, cheap booze, easily available weed and other drugs too if you can handle it."

"You sound like some kind of pusher," piped in Julie. She was English too; slim with dirty-blonde hair, and rather pulpy lips, which you could just image yourself sucking on.

Also present was Florent, a tall, very dark, black guy from Cameroun; Carlos, an Argentinean with a little goatee-beard; Nordeen, a matt-skinned, frizzy-haired Moroccan with little penny-rounder specs; Cho-May, an elegant Chinese girl; and Amber a bubbly American blonde.

I was impressed. This was definitely cosmopolitan.

* * *

We were all staying at the Deutsch de la Meurthe residence on the Cité Université campus in the south of Paris. This was one of the coolest 'houses' – as they called the residences there, since it had people of all nationalities, unlike most of the other houses which were dedicated to people of the same nationality: the British house, the Spanish house, the Argentinean house and so on.

Once the year kicked off there were indeed parties by the truckload. Most houses had a regular official party night weekly or monthly, usually with live music or a DJ. The parties were either free or just ten or twenty francs to get in and usually included one or two drinks, extra drinks were cheap, too – usually around five francs. Then there were the room parties and student nights on other campuses; not to mention pubbing and clubbing in Paris, if you felt like spending a bit more cash.

To start off with, Bruce and I did everything together. But then he started seeing some French biker chick called Sandrine. She had long, jet-black hair, eyes made up like Kiss and was a total nymphomaniac from what Bruce told us. So when he was busy with her, I mostly hung out with Florent and Henry.

Henry hailed from the Bronx, New York. He was your typical 'black dude from the hood,' as he liked to refer to himself: athletic, into the groove, too cool for school and a ladies' man. Everyone called him Hendrix, not because he could actually play the guitar – he couldn't. It was a nickname given by some of his girlfriends, apparently due to the magic he could perform with his tongue! He used to alternate between three different styles: the sports or streetwear look, consisting of baggy jeans, t-shirts, baseball caps and expensive trainers; the yuppie or buppie look, consisting of flash shirts, trousers or suits; and the Afro look, consisting of freaky-coloured afro-shirts, wooden-bead necklaces and bracelets. He always appeared cool and confident, no matter which of the three styles he adopted.

And then there was Florent, a real African, from Cameroun, Africa. The antithesis of Hendrix in that he was just so uncool: cheap nondescript shirts or t-shirts, jeans and sandals, very clumsy, hopeless at sports and clueless with the ladies.

* * *

So one Friday, a couple of months into the school year, we were sitting in Henry's room, just the three of us, enjoying a Bacardi and coke – it was Henry's drink of choice, despite the fact that I ribbed him endlessly that it was a girl's drink.

"So shall we head over to the American house?" I proposed. There was a big party down in the basement on there that night.

"Yeah, man, let's do it," agreed Henry. "Check out the talent. See if it's up to much."

"What kind of girl you like, Henry?" asked Florent.

"Give me a black goddess sister, I can't resist her," he rapped, adding a few vocal beat-box noises.

"Ice Cube, right?" I knew the line from a tape I'd been listening to. I was going through a rap phase, encouraged by Henry who listened to a lot.

"Yep, brother," said Henry. "What about you, Flo? What get's your juices to flo, flo, flo?"

"Well, blondes actually," he said bashfully. "That Amber, she's so beautiful."

So it turned out that Florent was my antithesis too, in the sense that his ideal woman was a white blonde – jungle fever in reverse. He spent the whole year fantasising over Amber and trying to pluck up the courage to make a move on her.

"Eh, what?" Henry looked flabbergasted. "Come on, man, you need to keep it Nubian!"

"Nah, white women are so beautiful, delicate and sensuous, like Marilyn Monroe, eh, Sandy?" Florent looked at me for support.

"Yeah, well they can be," I said. "But I have to agree with Henry. Black women are much sexier."

"Yeah, that's my man!" exclaimed Henry. "You ever make it with a black girl?"

"Well, now that you mention it, there was this one girl, Gabriella, in my high school."

"Ah-ha." Henry nodded knowingly. "Bet you've never looked back. We've got to get you fixed up again. Maybe at this party tonight. Beverly's going with some of her cute girlfriends. You can try hooking up with one of them."

Beverly was this curvaceous black girl from Los Angeles, who Henry was seeing on and off, so to speak – he didn't want to be tied down to one woman. If her friends were anywhere near as sexy as her, this night could be promising.

"As for you, you hopeless case," he said looking at Flo. "Good luck with Amber, you'll need it."

"Think she'll be there tonight?" asked Flo.

"No doubt," said Henry disdainfully. "Along with her stringy-haired Barbie doll friends."

We headed to the party around ten p.m. The thumping of the music could be heard from outside the residence. You showed your student card, and paid twenty francs at the door to get in. They gave you a little ticket which allowed you one drink; after that, you paid ten francs for a beer or wine, five francs for soft drinks. We all got beers then headed down into the basement where hundreds of people were swaying to the loud dance music.

Florent immediately clocked Amber and her pals and went over to dance with them. Henry and I played it cool for a bit, then he spotted Beverly, who was there with two friends. Beverly introduced us to them: Jade – another African American and Emilie – who was from Guadeloupe. Jade was the nicer looking, but seemed rather aloof, so I chatted to Emilie in French. I was glad to practise my French since I felt I hung out too much with Americans and Brits.

"So where d'you stay, Emilie?" I enquired.

"Here, in the American house," she replied.

"How did you wrangle that?"

"Well actually, they have a few places for non-Americans."

"Okay. Cool. You just here for a year like me?"

"No, I'm doing my studies here. French literature. Four year degree, then maybe I'll stay on to work."

"Don't you miss the Caribbean, you know, all the palm trees, dancing around in grass skirts?"

"Ha! Is it true you Scotsmen wear a skirt with nothing underneath?"

This seemed to fascinate a lot of French people. "Maybe I'll wear mine one day and you can find out for yourself," I said winking at her.

"Ooh!"

The current was passing between us. We went to dance. Her lithe body rubbed against me on the dance floor, and soon we were kissing. I noticed Henry was similarly engaged with Beverly. Florent wasn't having so much luck; the way he danced put paid to the myth that all black people have rhythm in their skin. Poor guy – I could see Amber and some of her Barbie doll friends rolling their eyes at his jerky, out of time movements on the floor.

Around one a.m. the party was still going strong, but Emilie took my hand and whispered in my ear, "Come and have some rum up in my room."

I followed her willingly. Henry noticed us leaving and gave me a knowing nod. Emilie led me up the stairs to her room on the top floor. She served two glasses of Guadeloupe rum, with just a squeeze of lemon and a sugar cube in each one. It was strong stuff; none of your Bacardi nonsense.

We kissed ever more fervently and began taking off each other's clothes.

"So do you think of yourself as African in any way?" I asked her.

"No. I'm French. Now just shut up and come here, you big Scottish hunk." She pulled me over to her bed.

It had been over two years since Gabriella. I was ready.

She moaned loudly as we made love to the distant beats of the music coming from the party.

* * *

We became an 'item' after that night. Henry was still going out with Beverly. Even Florent had managed to score with Amber. So for a while our little group split up, each of us mostly hanging out with our girlfriends. I would sleep over most nights at Emilie's room in the American house, or sometimes she'd come and stay over at mine. After a while it just became too stifling. I still fancied her, but there wasn't the same feeling of passion which I'd felt for Gabriella. I longed for my freedom, for a night out with the lads – no girlfriends tagging along.

Early in the New Year – 1991 – I managed to get free on a Thursday night. Emilie had some African dance class and I told her I'd just have a quiet night in studying. Then I managed to persuade Bruce and Henry to ditch their girlfriends for the night and come along to the jazz night at the Dutch house. Florent – still gaga about his blonde American – couldn't be swayed into coming.

We decided to splash out on a meal at the Spanish house. As we entered the restaurant, a cute little Latina girl just in front turned around, said 'Hola,' and winked at me, before continuing inside to join the queue. I'd noticed her a few times at the American house – she must have been in one of the rooms next to Emilie's, but I'd never really talked to her.

"You dog!" Henry muttered.

"What?" I protested. "I don't even know her name."

"Don't remember her name maybe, *cabrón*, but I bet you've been there!"

He and Bruce laughed.

After a hearty meal of paella, washed down with a couple of tins of beer, we headed up to the party at the Dutch house. The band was a classic set-up of a guitarist, a bass-guitarist, a drummer and a guy on keyboards. Instrumentals only, no singing. The guy on the drums was a very tall, white guy, with dreadlocks tied back with some Rasta-coloured headband and a long goatee-beard. After a couple of numbers it became clear that he was the real star of the band – he just dwarfed the others physically and especially musically. The guy was so hot, if you closed your eyes, it sounded as if there were three or four percussionists and not just one person. The place was busy, especially for a Thursday night and practically everyone was dancing or swaying to the music. After a while the drummer really took over the show, the other musicians contenting themselves with a basic backing, while he set the place on fire with his amazing drumming skills.

They eventually stopped for a break and we chatted about music, our courses and mostly about girls. Bruce told us in overly explicit details about his relationship with Sabrine and the other 'bits on the side' he'd had sex with 'just for the experience.'

"Come on, Sandy, you don't want to get tied down to one girl," he jibed. This is Erasmus man! Live the experience!"

"He's right brother," agreed Hendrix. "Make the most of it.

Black girls are the best of course, but you should play the field. Maybe try a French girl."

"Or an English one," said Bruce. "I think that Julie's into you, she's been not so discretely eyeing you up all night." He gave a little nod in her direction.

I looked over and there she was, standing with a group of her friends – mostly from the British house. She looked away coyly. Now normally, as a Scot, I wouldn't go for an English girl; old prejudices die hard against the 'auld enemy'. But I suppose part of going to university and going on Erasmus was opening up to people of all nationalities, colours and creeds; putting your prejudices aside and finding out for yourself what people were really like. Julie might have been English and not my 'type' but she was definitely cool and sexy. And into me apparently, so why not?

When the music started up, I went over to dance with her. There was a technique back then in parties and nightclubs where you would go and dance behind a girl and move in closer and closer. If she moved away, you knew she wasn't interested, that you'd misread the 'signals.' If, however, she allowed you to move in close, brushing against her, your hands maybe caressing her waist, you knew you were in there. That's how I proceeded with Julie. She allowed me to move in close to caress her waist, turning her head to smile at me now and then as we gyrated to the music.

The keyboardist and the guitarist had conceded defeat, leaving the stage to the bassist, the star-drummer and two other percussionists: a black guy on a djembé and a North African on a darbuka. The latter were apparently friends of the main drummer, whom he'd invited up to play. The rhythm became more and more enthralling, the crowd swirling and writhing, being transported to another place: Africa.

Julie and I caressed each other and kissed on the dance floor; her lips were so full and luscious, they drove me wild with desire. I was enveloped in the moment, intoxicated by the music, by her touch and her perfume. I forgot about Emilie, didn't feel guilty, and didn't really care if she found out – which she undoubtedly would – this was the main Thursday night party on campus, after all and it was likely that one of her friends or acquaintances was here and had seen us and would tell Emilie.

"So, Julie, your place or mine?" I asked her towards the end of the night.

"Yours, Sandy. It's closer." Julie took my hand and we headed off.

I nodded towards Henry and Bruce on the way out, who gave me little nods back and thumbs up.

Julie and I headed back to my room, where we let ourselves be consumed by our passions, making love three times before falling asleep in each other's arms. I could still hear the African beats in my head as I drifted off to sleep, somehow calling me to more experience, more passion, and more feeling.

* * *

So I went on to 'live the experience' as Bruce put it. Eyes and ears had indeed been present that night at the Dutch house. Emilie called me up the very next day, shouted "Bastard!" at me and then just slammed the phone down before I could reply. I had regular bouts with Julie during the rest of the school year, but unlike Emilie, she was in no way my 'girlfriend.' She was a nice girl, despite her Englishness; but we both knew, despite never saying it out loud, that it was just physical between us.

I also hooked up with the little Latina girl who'd winked at me – Gisella; got talking to her one night at the Spanish house restaurant and finished up with tequilas and sex back in her room, which was indeed just next to Emilie's in the American house. She was Peruvian and a total party animal. Sex for her was incidental, all she wanted to do was dance from dusk till dawn, in the parties and nightclubs of France's capital. She took me to big student parties, preferably with Latino music, Latino bars and clubs like the Queen and the Locomotive. Being with her was fun, exciting and wild, but also a bit exhausting, not to mention a strain on my limited student wallet.

"Come on, Sandy!" she'd whoop over the loud nightclub music. "You only live once!"

Yeah, but you might not live that long at this rate, I felt like saying.

Chapter 8

I Once Knew a Girl Called Maria

To complicate matters even more, I 'took on' a third woman at the same time: Maria. I met her one Thursday night in April, at a salsa night Gisella (who else?) had invited me to. She was there with her husband; yes she was *married* although not happily apparently. Gisella knew them and introduced us. She was Brazilian, a gorgeous Métis of black and white and maybe South American Indian; full lips and big, brown eyes, which held my gaze when we were introduced. I was immediately captivated by her beauty. We chatted a bit, all four of us, drank beers and tequilas and danced – it was mostly salsa, which you dance with a partner. On some dances we switched partners, Gisella dancing with Friedrich – Maria's rather uptight Austrian husband, and me with Maria. I could feel the warmth emanating from her. At one point she whispered in my ear, "I can feel something between us." I just smiled, not really encouragingly – her husband was there after all – but not discouragingly either.

Friedrich had to leave early, around midnight, since he had work the next day. I had lectures of course, but that wasn't really work, and if you missed them you could always get photocopies and catch up later. Around four-thirty Gisella announced she was going with a group of friends, and others she'd met that night, to an 'after' at some place called the Rexy. I guess she wasn't aiming to attend the next morning's or even afternoon's lectures. She tried to persuade Maria and me to come too. I said no, with the excuse of lectures the next morning. Maria just said she had to get the first metro home. So Gisella headed off with her group and I was left alone with Maria.

"Alone at last," she said, looking at me suggestively, holding my hand under the table we were sitting at.

My heart was beating with attraction, but also with guilt. My Catholic conscience was strained enough sleeping around with single girls, but to go with a married woman – that was full-on adultery.

"What about your husband?"

"I don't love him anymore. I'm going to leave him soon."

I didn't know what to say. For Catholics divorce was a big no-no. "Can't you resolve your differences?"

"All he likes is beer and football. We married too young. I want someone who will treat me like a woman, you know, with love and tenderness." She put her head on my shoulder. "Someone like you."

I felt guiltily aroused. "Anyway, let's head off. It's almost time for the first metro."

"Have one last dance with me, Sandy."

She pulled me up to the dance floor.

It was a slow number and she held me close. I could feel the warmth of her body, smell the enticing aroma of her perfume.

We caught the metro to her stop – Porte d'Orleans. It was handily within walking distance of my residence at the Cité Universitaire. It was six a.m. by the time I walked her to the foot of her apartment building. She jotted her number on a scrap of paper.

"Call me, sometime during the day when Friedrich's out," she said. "He'll never know."

Then she kissed me fully on the lips, a promise of what was to come if I did call her.

I broke off from her kiss. "I'd better not. Bye, Maria."

"Call me," she repeated.

I walked back to my room, slept for about three hours, then made it in for the second lecture of the day at ten. Maria's perfume still lingering on me as a sign of my guilt.

* * *

When I told the lads about Maria, their advice was contradictory.

"Stay away from married women," said Henry. "Trust me." Despite his reputation as a 'player,' Henry did have a strict moral code.

"She's more or less given you an invitation to come by for sex during the day," said Bruce. "Seize the opportunity. Call her you idiot! If you don't, give me the number and I'll do her." *Ever the sleaze ball.* Bruce's moral code was non-existent.

Florent was more philosophical. He'd come back into our 'gang' when the love of his life, Amber, had left after the first semester, and was trying against all odds to keep the relationship going long-distance. "Let love rule, my friend. Maybe her first marriage was a mistake. Maybe she's the one for you."

So, angel, devil or somewhere in between? Which was I going to be?

At first, I tried the angel path. Well angel to a point – I kept on sleeping with Gisella and Julie. But no calling Maria; trying to forget her.

A couple of weeks after my encounter with her, I'd just had sex with Gisella and she came out with, "So what happened between you and Maria? Apparently she's quite taken with you."

"Oh, nothing," I said. "She's married anyway. Out of bounds."

"Don't be so old fashioned. Anyway her marriage is on its last legs. Why don't you give her a shot? She wants to see you again. Been asking for your number, where you live."

"What? I hope you didn't tell her?"

"No, but still."

* * *

I found out what 'but still' meant the next weekend, when Gisella invited me out to a house party and Maria just happened to be there.

She cornered me in the kitchen at one point. "Sandy, how

come you haven't called me yet? I've been waiting."

"Well you know, busy with this and that. Plus there's your husband."

"I told you *cariño*, our marriage is more or less over. I want *you*." She caressed my arm. "And guess what," she added mischievously. "He's away this weekend and all next week – off to Austria for a family visit and work."

"Ah, I see, right." I felt my resistance caving in as she gazed lasciviously into my eyes.

We left the party early together. Gisella winked knowingly at me as we said our goodbyes.

We spent the rest of that night and most of the remaining weekend having sex back at her apartment, insatiable for each other. I continued going to her house every evening, while her husband was away, feeling every bit the 'dog' that Henry had called me, a mixture of guilt and excitement.

At the end of the week, she persuaded me to give her my phone number. Told me she'd call me when the coast was clear. She wanted my address, too.

"That way I could come round to yours sometimes," she pleaded. "It would be easier."

I thought it wiser to refuse. "I prefer coming here, Maria. We're not supposed to have overnight visitors." This was true but not enforced, in our residence or any of the others on campus.

So I continued seeing her, when she gave me a call to say I could come over. When the courses ended and the examination period began, I was free during the day, unless I had an exam; so I would sometimes even go over in the morning, just after her husband had left for work. Maria wasn't currently in employment. She began proclaiming her love for me, listing all her husband's faults, how she wanted to leave him for me. I felt an overpowering physical attraction for her (*control your lusts!*) but wasn't sure about 'love,' wasn't sure if I even knew what it meant. Had I loved Gabriella? I still thought about her. How did my feelings for Maria compare? Maybe if she'd been single it would have been different. I didn't want to be the home breaker.

"Remember I have to go back to Scotland after this school year," I tried to reason with her. "Can't we just enjoy the moment?"

"I could come with you to Scotland, Sandy. I love you. You're the man of my life."

This was getting serious.

Once I was in the thick of the exams, the last three weeks in June, I decided to stop seeing her, at least until the final assessments were over.

"I need a break, to concentrate on my revision," I told her. "Just the next three weeks."

"*Three weeks!*" She made it sound like an eternity. "And then you'll be going back to Scotland, won't you! You're going to just leave me!"

"No, Maria, it's not like that. Anyway, I've applied for a few summer jobs. I'll probably be staying on in Paris until at least the end of September."

* * *

Maria continued to call me every day during the exam-break. The assessments went fine and there were the end of year parties: boozing with my new Erasmus friends, exchanging addresses, promising to write and to visit, but knowing deep down that I'd never see most of them again. I'd managed to get a summer job with a big industrialist called Schlumberger. Practically all my friends were leaving Paris though, at the end of June or beginning of July; only Henry and Gisella were staying on – they'd both found summer jobs like me.

Maria, of course, knew that I'd finished all my exams and that I'd found a summer job, and started hassling me to come over, to pick up where we'd left off. I decided this was the time to make a clean break. I had to leave the Deutsch de la Meurthe residence the first week in July and I'd found a place at the American house for the summer. So had Henry. This was ideal for us since both Beverly and Gisella were staying on there for the summer too. I just wanted to do my summer job, go drinking with Henry, screw Gisella whenever she was up for it and forget Maria – too complicated, too serious and too much guilt. I made Gisella promise not to tell her where I was staying or my new telephone number.

"You're such a scoundrel," she said. "The poor girl's besotted with you. Why can't you just let her down gently if you want out?"

"Easier said than done. I just want a clean break."

She reluctantly agreed to keep mum about my whereabouts.

* * *

Two weeks into July, I was settled into the American house. The summer job was boring but at least paid enough to cover my rent and food with a little money leftover for partying. I thought that Maria had accepted our severance, but I was badly mistaken. There was a knock at my door early one Sunday morning. Six a.m! I was just going to ignore it, but then they knocked again, harder.

I opened the door, and there was Maria, holding the hand of a little boy – he must have been about two years old.

Her eyes were all red – I could see she'd been crying. "Maria! What's the matter? What are you doing here? And who's this?" I indicated the boy, who immediately started wailing.

She didn't reply to any of my questions but made her way into my room, sat down on the bed and began comforting the boy.

"So this is where you live now? Why didn't you tell me you'd moved and changed telephone number? I've been trying to get a hold of you. I've done it, Sandy. I've left Friedrich. We can be together now. Oh, my love!" She burst into tears and came over to hold me.

I tried to soothe her. "It's okay, Maria. What happened?"

Once she'd calmed down a little she told me the whole story. Last night she'd had a big argument with Friedrich and had blurted out that she was seeing someone else. They'd disputed until the early hours of the morning, Friedrich becoming more and more aggressive, eventually smashing things in their apartment and punching holes in the walls. Fearing that he would start hitting her, she hastily packed a bag and left, with little Alanyo, her son. She'd gone to Gisella's room, who'd broken her promise, giving in to Maria's beseeching and told her where I lived.

"You never told me you had a son." I nodded towards the boy, who'd fallen asleep on the bed.

"I'm sorry, Sandy. It just never came up. He's been staying with Friedrich's parents in Austria for a couple of months, while we tried to mend our marriage, but it's no use, it's broken beyond repair."

Never came up! How could the fact that you have a son never come up? I wanted to say, but I just stared at her shaking my head in shock.

"Please, Sandy, let us stay with you," she looked into my eyes pleadingly. "Take us back to Scotland with you. I know we can make this work. You're the man of my dreams."

"You can stay for a few days, until you find another place. But Scotland… no way! Be serious, Maria. I'm a penniless student. I've still another year of my studies to complete."

"We'll talk about it later, Sandy. We can work something out." She began to kiss me. "I'm sorry, Sandy. Waking you up so early and everything. I've missed you so much."

She made a little makeshift bed on the floor for Alanyo with some blankets and towels and then came back to bed with me, where I gave in to her physical advances. We made love passionately then, exhausted, she fell asleep almost immediately in my arms. I took longer getting back to sleep. What had I got myself into?

Chapter 9

Riding the Locomotive

The Erasmus dream experience of partying and non-committal sex was turning into a nightmare.

"I told you, man," said Henry shaking his head. "Stay away from married women! Now you have two choices: step up or step away. I know which I'd choose – the latter."

"How can I step away?" I asked. "She's taken up residence in my room with her kid and is talking about coming back to Scotland with me."

"Just tell her to go back to her husband. That kid ain't your responsibility."

"I've tried that. She says she's frightened of him; that he might beat her up."

"She could call the police or social services. Don't get involved," he advised. "Otherwise you may be the one getting beat up by the cuckold husband. It could get messy, even messier than it is now. Why don't you just get another girlfriend, then she'll get the message."

"Another girlfriend?" I asked incredulously. "You think that's going to make things less messy?"

"Sure, think about it. She's in love with you. She thinks you feel the same. What better way to make her face up to reality. Let's go clubbing this weekend and hook up with some new girls."

I let myself be persuaded and we made plans to go to the Locomotive – legendry Parisian nightclub and one of the few places that had decent music, good talent and to which we had a chance of getting in.

* * *

So when Saturday night arrived, I told Maria I was going out for a few drinks with Henry. She protested, asking suspiciously if I was going to see another woman – the famous female intuition. I promised her it would be just me and Henry, getting him to come round and knock on my door, to reassure her.

"Be good!" She said giving me a hard stare as we left.

We went back to his room first for beers and Bacardis. As I knocked back the first shot of Bacardi, I closed my eyes and imagined that this was back at the start of the Erasmus trip, two single student guys on a Saturday night: drinking, partying, off to a nightclub, trying to get laid. How much simpler it had been back then.

Henry read my mind. "This is going to be just like back at the start of the year. You'll see, we're going to have fun man! Paris by night! We're going to get wrecked, we're going to dance with tasty babes and we're going to score!"

That was the plan anyway.

Once we'd finished the beers and most of the Bacardi, we went to one of our Irish pub haunts for pints in the marais quarter, from about ten till midnight. You didn't want to get to the club too early, since it only started getting busy around midnight and it was better to get a skinful of cheap booze first, to avoid paying the extortionate prices once you got inside. Henry managed to buy some hash off a Rastafarian guy in the men's room and we made joints and smoked them round the back of the pub between pints. You could still smoke in bars in those days, but wacky backy – with its unmistakable smell – would get you kicked out for sure.

We got the metro to Pigalle, then made the short walk to the club, ignoring the people that would try to entice you into the seedy sex clubs, which the area was famous for. I suddenly started to have serious doubts about us getting into the club. We were both rather drunk, especially Henry, who must have been on the Bacardis even before he picked me up. Not only that but he had stupidly chosen to wear one of his freaky coloured afro-shirts.

"It's tough enough getting into this place as it is, without you dressing up like some African dictator," I chided him

"That is just *so* racist!" he retorted.

"Yes, well, nightclub bouncers aren't exactly renowned for their political correctness. Let's use the trick of joining the queue after a group of girls!" I proposed.

"Okay, my man!"

The idea was to join the queue after a group of girls, chat them up a bit, and ask them to go along with the scenario that we were all together – if challenged by the bouncer. That and try and look sensible and sober; a bit difficult after all the booze and weed we'd consumed.

We noticed two sassily dressed young girls, one black and one white, near the club and subtly followed them as they joined the queue. It seemed that the gods were with us: they went along with our plan and we invited them for a drink once inside.

The white girl was called Katy; she had dark hair and tanned skin. She wore a figure hugging red mini-dress.

The black one introduced herself as Roquelle, "Call me Rocky – you know, like the boxer!"

"I wouldn't mind going a few rounds with you," I quipped and she laughed.

I warmed to her immediately. She was sexily dressed in a sparkling black mini-dress, which showed off her beautiful long legs. She looked a lot like Gabriella: slender body with curves in all the right places, enchanting eyes and dazzling smile. She was a beautiful African pearl from the Ivory Coast, even the name of her country somehow exotic, enticing and full of the promise of adventure.

Taking my cue, Hendrix made his move on Katy and she seemed to be responding. We had vodka and orange juices at the bar, then headed to the mainstream dance floor. The Locomotive was great in that it had three massive dance floors – one on each of the three separate levels: basement was soul, R&B and hip-hop; ground level was mainstream pop and dance music; upper level was rock. So if you didn't like the music, the scene, the talent on one level, you could just move and see what was going on, on one of the other levels.

That night the place was buzzing: great music, sexy women, everyone going wild on the dance floor. Boozed and hashed up, testosterone flowing with the promise of subsequent sex, I felt limitless, elated, like I was soaring.

Later during the night, we were dancing down in the basement to James Brown, Marvin Gaye, the Blues Brothers; then they put on some 'zouk' music and Rocky showed me how to dance to it: our bodies hugging each other, legs interlaced – it seemed about the closest you could be to having sex with your clothes still on.

The real sex came later. We all left at five and got the metro and RER back to the American house. Henry invited us to his room for a Bacardi and coke.

"Can't we go to your room?" Rocky whispered in my ear. Henry and Katy were already necking and fondling each other on top of his bed.

"No. I have a room-mate who's really uptight," I remained vague. "Let's just stay here."

We put down a camping sleeping mat and some blankets on the floor – and began embracing and caressing each other. It felt weird doing it in the same room as Henry and Katy – there was just a desk between our makeshift bed and their bed. I was so aroused though by Rocky's soft skin and firm body that any inhibitions I may have had were quickly suppressed. As we made love I could hear the other two going at it – it was almost like an orgy. I suddenly thought of the book from back in my school, with the witches and warlocks and orgy scenes, and perversely imagined I was taking part – this turned me on even more.

After the lovemaking, the three of them all fell asleep, but I was troubled by thoughts of that book and then suddenly I remembered – Ivory Coast – that was where Gabriella had come from; not my Gabriella, the other one, the disgraced nun. Strange coincidence. The warnings of the nun, Bernadette, came back to me. "Forget Gabriella, forget African women, avoid them at all costs… The witches, African devil worshippers… Try and control your *lusts!*" She would be turning in her grave if she could see me now, at the peak of my year of being ruled by my lusts rather than attempting to control them in any way, sleeping with an African woman I'd just met that night. This pure beauty by my side a devil worshipper? Hardly likely. I gazed at Rocky as she slept peacefully beside me; she wore a golden chain with a cross around her neck, which reassured me somewhat. Bernadette was obviously deranged. Maybe she'd been jealous of Gabriella and Andy. She might have been in love with him or even her – I'm sure a lot of nuns are closet lesbians; who knows what goes on in these convents and in the minds of the women who live there. Maybe she'd even set the fire. Would I ever know the truth? Perhaps if I could speak to Andy, he'd shed some light on the matter.

I eventually fell into a restless sleep, which lasted a couple of hours. Then Rocky woke me to say that she and Katy, were leaving.

"Why don't you stay a bit longer?" I asked her. It was only nine a.m.

"I have to get back home. I'm going to church with my family," she explained. "Told them I was staying over at Katy's and that I'd be back this morning."

So, she was definitely not a devil worshipper. Off to repent in church for this night of debauchery.

"Can we see each other again?" I asked.

"Yes I'd like that." She smiled.

We exchanged telephone numbers and the girls left. Henry

didn't even wake up; apparently for him and Katy it was strictly a one-night stand.

* * *

Maria was not happy when I eventually showed up back at my room later that morning.

"Where were you?" she asked accusingly.

"Well, we got back a bit late. I just slept at Henry's. Didn't want to wake you and little Alanyo."

"Yeah right, I can smell the perfume on you," she said grabbing my t-shirt and sniffing it. "You've been with another woman haven't you?"

There was no point in denying it. In fact, the point was actually that she should find out. "Well what if I was. Come on, Maria, you have to face up to it. We're not going to stay together. When I go back to Scotland, that's it. I really think you should just go back to Friedrich and try and patch things up."

"Patch things up? Are you mad? The guy could have killed me the other night."

"Don't exaggerate. He was just upset. Who wouldn't be after what you did."

"Oh great, take his side why don't you. Don't forget I left him for *you!*"

She broke down crying. I went to comfort her but she pushed me away. Then Alanyo, who had been napping, woke up and started crying too. *Great!* I picked him up to soothe him, gave him a biscuit and he soon calmed down.

"See how he likes you," said Maria. "I think you'd be a great dad to him."

"Oh *please*! The wee guy needs his real dad, to get back to his home, not to be staying here in some cramped student room."

She had actually installed a little travel cot for him, brought some of his toys; if truth be told, the boy was making himself at home and didn't seem to be missing his dad at all. But I had to stand firm.

"I'd like to get on with my life," I pursued. "I may start seeing this other girl a bit."

"You're just using her to try and get rid of me, you creep." It was amazing how quickly she could see my little plan. "*Vira homem!*" Be a man!

After she got over her tears, she calmed down and made us a delicious lunch of rice and beans. She wasn't going anywhere and proceeded to dote on me as if nothing had happened, even having sex with me that very night. Make up sex, I suppose in her mind. Even though I wanted her gone I couldn't resist her advances.

* * *

What could I do but stick to the plan and try and show her that I had a new girlfriend. I called Rocky on Monday and arranged to see her on Wednesday night. I didn't say anything to Maria and just caught the metro into Paris directly from work. We met in a bar – the aptly named Hideout in the Châtelet district. I knew the place well since it had one of the cheapest and longest happy hours in Paris.

"So what'll it be? Whisky on the Rocks?" I joked.

"I'll go for a white wine," she said.

I went for the traditional pint of lager.

We sat down at a table and chinked glasses.

"So, great night on Saturday, eh?" I said.

"Yes," she agreed. "Shame we couldn't be somewhere a bit more intimate together after though."

"Well hopefully my room-mate will be moving out soon, so we'll have the place to ourselves." Wishful thinking on my part.

"It's a woman isn't it? She's your girlfriend right?" More uncanny female mind reading.

"Yes, it's true," I owned up. "Ex-girlfriend really. She's about to leave. I've told her it's over. Otherwise I wouldn't be here with you. Any chance we could go to yours in the meantime?"

"No way! I live with my aunt and uncle – strict Catholics remember."

She'd told me this on Saturday. She was a student nurse, but unlike the nurses I knew in Glasgow, she didn't have an in-hospital room. She stayed in the suburbs of Paris with her aunt, Odette, Odette's husband, Charles and their two children, Rocky's younger cousins: a boy and a girl who were both still in secondary school.

"They're strictly no sex before marriage," she continued. "Hard line Catholics."

"Like mine," I said. "One of the reasons I chose to study away from home."

"I'm glad you did. Glad you made it to Paris. So we could meet."

We drank, kissed and felt each other up until around ten, when the happy hour ended, then went for a pizza in a nearby Italian restaurant. I wanted to be with her *so* much. Even though she was just supposed to be a way of getting rid of Maria, I was beginning to fall for her. She was so exquisitely beautiful and charming.

I was longing to be with her again, but we parted around midnight down in the Châtelet-les-Halles RER suburban train station. She was getting the A line, me the B.

"What's your family name by the way?" I asked her.

"Coste. C-O-S-T-E. And yours?"

"Beech. B-E-E-C-H."

Sandy Beech and Rocky Coste – a match made in heaven.

"So, Mister Beech, shall we meet up again at the weekend?"

"Sure! I look forward to exploring the Rocky Coste a bit more next time." I joked.

"I look forward to more fun on the Sandy Beech!" She winked at me.

I couldn't wait.

If only I could find a way to get Maria and her kid to move out.

* * *

Henry proposed a visit to the catacombs on Saturday afternoon. After a year living in Paris, I'd done all the main sights: Eiffel Tower, Sacre Coeur, Notre Dame, Louvre, Musée d'Orsay, Centre Pompidou, Versailles; and some of the lesser known ones: Marmottan Monet museum, Arab Institute, Musée de l'Homme and of course Père Lachaise cemetery, where I'd visited the tomb of the legendary Jim Morrison of the Doors. I'd heard of the catacombs of course, having read about it in guide books and in the 'Officiel' magazine – a weekly what's on guide I often bought for a few centimes. It was described as an underground necropolis (*remember Glasgow!*) containing the remains of over six million people, mostly removed from other, overflowing cemeteries in the late eighteenth century and early nineteenth. I'd frankly thought of the place as less of a 'must-see' and more of a 'better to avoid.'

"It'll be awesome, dude, the biggest necropolis in the world; creepy underground passageways, like something from an Indiana Jones movie." He really talked the place up.

"A collection of peoples' bones, disrespectfully removed from their original graveyards, stacked up in dusty claustrophobic corridors, and put on display for our macabre amusement. It's just not right, sacrilegious even."I replied.

"You know what I think about God and religions." He'd already expressed his atheistic views on several occasions.

"Morbid then. Shouldn't we just let the dead rest in peace?"

"Come on, man, don't be such a square," he chided me.

I eventually agreed to accompany him on the visit, despite my better judgement. At least I got a favour out of him: he gave me the keys for his room on Friday night, so I could sleep with Rocky, while he went off to Beverly's room.

Friday evening, Rocky came for a meal on campus. I took her to the Spanish house, then we frolicked on the grass – kissing ever more ardently and rolling on top of each other while the sun set. Then I took her back to Henry's room and we made mad passionate love.

The next morning I didn't really fancy going back to my room to face Maria's accusations. I'd already brought spare clothes and toiletries to Henry's room, so it wasn't as if I needed to go back right away. Rocky had brought an overnight bag too. So we just showered, changed and took a walk around campus, before grabbing sandwiches and eating them outside on the big lawn.

"Got anything planned for the rest of the weekend?" I asked her.

"Well nothing today, but you know, the usual family Sunday – church and so on," she replied.

"Fancy coming to visit the catacombs," I proposed. "I'm going with Henry later this afternoon."

"Ooh! The catacombs – a bit scary, so I've heard. Okay, why not. At least we can hang out a bit longer together today. Then I'll probably head back home for dinner with the family."

Henry met us back at his room around two p.m. and off we went – it was just one stop on the RER to Denfert-Rochereau.

The visit was just as macabre as I had feared.

We walked down steps until we were twenty metres underground – into what used to be a stone mine. After a small museum section explaining the history of the place, there was a gallery containing sculptures, carved directly out of the stone. I noted with trepidation that the sculptor – a certain Décure, alias 'Beauséjour', which ironically means 'nice stay' – was killed when he attempted to create a stairway to an upper level of the quarry and provoked a cave-in.

Then we went into the actual ossuary, which had a plaque at

the entrance reading 'Stop! This is the empire of death.' Once inside there were human skulls and bones everywhere, from floor to ceiling, sometimes 'artistically' arranged, other times just indiscriminately stacked up. There were plaques telling where the bones were from and when they were inhumed in the catacombs. For example, 'Bones from the cemetery of the innocent deposited in April 1786.' Other plaques offered quotations from the Bible, or from famous poets such as Dante and Desmartin, or ominous warnings. 'Whichever way you turn death is watching you,' was the one that marked me the most, as it seemed to describe the eerie way in which the skulls appeared to be staring at us, as we made our way along the passageways.

Henry and Rocky didn't seem as affected as I was, fingering the bones and skulls throughout the visit. At one point Henry even lay on top of one of the stone altars, crossed two tibia bones over his chest, then hissed in a mock evil tone, "Awaken, Nosferatu!"

"Cut it out!" I chided him. "Have you no respect for the dead?"

He just smirked back at me.

Rocky also played the joker at one point, holding up a skull and quoting from Hamlet, "Alas, poor Yorick! I knew him, Horatio."

They both guffawed. I just shook my head and rolled my eyes. Hopeless cases the pair of them. I was surprised, though, that Rocky could correctly quote from Shakespeare. Her English was amazing.

Despite their joking I was glad to get out of the place, the whole atmosphere weighed heavily on me. At the exit they actually frisked us down to make sure we hadn't stolen anything. There was a little display showing the bones and even a skull that people had tried to smuggled out.

"What, you mean someone actually tried to walk out of here with a skull?" I asked the security guy incredulously.

"Yes, you'd be surprised," he answered.

We all went for a drink after in a nearby bar; I needed one after that place.

"How'd you learn to speak English so well?" I questioned Rocky, steering the conversation away from what we'd just seen.

"From school, plus I did a six month exchange trip to London," she replied.

"Impressive!" I complemented her. "My French is nowhere near as good, even after a year here. And Henry here, he can still hardly string two words together." I nodded towards him.

"Cheeky!" he replied. "Anyway French is irrelevant in the world today. English dominates. USA! USA!"

I just sighed.

"I could never live here," he continued. "Jeez, just look at how they treat their dead people."

Just look at how you treat them, I felt like saying, but held my tongue.

"What about you, Sandy?" asked Rocky. "Could you live here?" She looked at me rather seductively. *'Would you come and live with me?'* was what she was really asking.

"Yes," I replied. "Why not? I kind of like it here. There's always something going on, something to do." *I kind of like you.*

We just had a couple of drinks, then Rocky headed home and Henry and I decided to go for a Chinese meal in the thirteenth district – Paris's Chinatown.

"You lucky dog," said Henry. "What a stunner. I can see why you'd want to come back to Paris."

"Yes. Thanks for letting us use your room last night."

"No problems. Any time, man. Although you have to stand firm against that Maria. Does she know you're seeing someone else?"

"Yes, I told her. But she's still not budging. I feel sorry for her, what with her kid and everything. But it wasn't like I told her to bust up with her husband or move out."

"Yes, or move in with you. Totally brazen. She's trying to get you through guilt, well that and via your loins obviously." He laughed.

"What about you and Beverly? You going to keep seeing her when you get back to the US?"

"Nah, I doubt it. It was good fun while it lasted. Anyway, she's in LA and I'm NYC – long distance relationships never last."

What about Rocky and me? Would our relationship last when I moved back to Scotland after the end of summer? Could I score a job over here and move back to be with her in a year, once I'd finished my studies? Only time would tell.

* * *

Maria welcomed me back to my room with a glower when I arrived around twelve midnight.

"Where have you been?" she interrogated me. "I haven't seen you since Friday morning."

"Oh just out and about," I replied nonchalantly. "Went for a chinky with Hendrix."

"You've been with *her* again haven't you?" she said accusingly.

I didn't answer.

"What do I have to do to convince you that I'm the one for you?" she continued, softening her tone. "We could be a great little family – you, me, Alanyo and maybe another little baby when we're ready."

A baby! That was the last thing on my mind, but that night I had dreams, or nightmares rather, of a wailing baby. We made love of course – I still found Maria as sexy as ever and couldn't resist her advances, but the last thing I thought about before falling asleep was those staring skulls down in the catacombs. My nightmare was about roaming around among the bones and the skulls, trying to find out where the distressed sounds of the baby were coming from. Then suddenly I realised that the sounds were real. I awoke and found little Alanyo standing up in his cot and crying; not just crying but screaming as if he were being attacked. Maria was tossing and turning in her sleep – having a nightmare too perhaps – but she didn't awake, so I took the little lad in my arms and comforted him, calmed him down and put him back to sleep in his cot. It did make me feel somewhat fatherly, protective and gentle. Could I really be a dad to this little boy? It would mean sacrifices of course, giving up the life of a roaming, selfish bachelor but maybe it was time to settle down. I'd sewn my wild oats enough during this one year in Paris, that was for sure.

Such selfless thoughts were soon forgotten though. Alanyo kept on waking up, each time screaming louder and louder; each time it was me that had to get up to calm him, Maria wouldn't awaken even when I called her and shook her hard. I tried feeding him, taking his temperature, listening to his breathing and his heartbeat, even looking inside his mouth to see if he was teething – physically everything seemed fine.

"What's wrong, wee guy?" I asked as I consoled him. He seemed to be looking over at the window, as if frightened of something out there.

"Come on, pal, it's okay, there's nothing out there." I took him over and had a look out – it was deathly silent outside. However, this didn't reassure him at all, if anything his screams intensified.

"Okay, okay, pal." I moved away from the window. His big eyes seemed to be trying to communicate with me. "If only you could speak and tell me what's wrong."

Around eight in the morning, Maria finally awoke.

"What's wrong with Alanyo?" she asked. "He never usually cries like this."

"At last you're awake," I said. I felt totally harrowed. "He's been like this all night while you slept. I've tried everything. Maybe you should take him to see a doctor."

"Oh God, I'm so worried! What's wrong with him? Please

come with us to the doctor," she begged me.

It was the least I could do. We managed to find a clinic that was open on Sunday and got there as quickly as we could. By the time we were in the waiting room though he had chirped up and was actually smiling and laughing. The doctor gave him a clean bill of health and me a hefty bill of two hundred francs.

The weather was sunny and beautiful, so I let Maria talk me into spending the day outside with them. We got baguettes, cheese, cold meat, fruit, juice and water and went for a picnic in the Parc Monsouris – a big park just opposite the Cité Universitaire. After eating, we all had a siesta on the grass. Due to the virtually sleepless night I'd just had, I could have slept all afternoon, but after a couple of hours Alanyo woke up and we took him to feed the ducks on the little lake, then to the children's play area where he had a great time playing on the swing, the chute, the roundabout, etc. A blissful 'family' outing.

"Thank you, Sandy, for taking care of us," said Maria towards the end of the afternoon.

That's what she wanted – someone to take care of her and the boy. All I wanted was out; no matter how much she turned me on, I couldn't be doing with bringing up someone else's kid. One night practically without sleep had given me a small taste of the domestic hell which awaited me if I went along with her.

We wound up the day with takeaway pizzas on the big lawn of the Cité Universitaire.

As soon as we got back to the room, around nine p.m. Alanyo started crying again. Maria rocked him and finally got him to sleep around ten. Then we went to bed too. I was so exhausted we didn't even have sex. Then about half an hour after going to bed, just as I was dropping off to sleep, the kid started screaming blue murder again. *Oh, no,* I thought to myself, *don't tell me this is going to be a repeat of last night!* It certainly looked that way; Maria was yet again in a deep sleep and couldn't be woken, so I got up to try and calm the boy down.

Just like the previous night, he seemed to be looking fearfully towards the window. I took him over and forced him to look out. It was perfectly safe; the window was open but, like a lot of ground-floor places in Paris, there were bars on the outside to dissuade thieves. "Look, Alanyo, there's nothing out there, nothing to be afraid of," I said to him. "Please just calm down."

He began writhing in my arms. He kicked out at the plant that was sitting on the inner window ledge and I caught a glimpse of something that had been leaning against the plant pot – on the window side – falling out of the window. It looked like a piece of bone; disturbingly like one of the old pieces of skull from the catacombs! Or was my mind just playing tricks on me? It could have just been a bone from one of the meals we'd eaten – chicken, beef, lamb – that someone had stashed there, too lazy to go to the bin. I couldn't look out of the window to the ground below to get a close look because of the bars and I wasn't about to go wandering around in the dark looking for it. I promised myself I'd go outside and have a look the next day.

Bizarrely, as soon as the bone – or whatever it was – fell out of the window, Alanyo calmed down and in a couple of minutes he was asleep in my arms. Nevertheless, I decided to shut the window. We usually kept it open all the time because of the heat; Paris that summer was stifling and the temperature remained high even during the night. Thankfully, Alanyo slept peacefully for the rest of the night. I tossed and turned for a while, I had a strange feeling in my guts that something was just not right, but after a while I eventually got to sleep, too.

When I left for work the next morning, I had a quick look outside below the window, there was nothing to be seen. Maybe it had fallen down the drain which was below the window or a stray cat had made off with it; or maybe the whole thing had been in my imagination, my sleep-deprived brain playing tricks on me. I did note that if I reached up I could easily place something beside the plant pot, if the window were open. An insane thought crossed my mind. Did someone place some cursed bone from the catacombs on my window ledge just in order to frighten little Alanyo? No, that was just madness. A piece of chicken bone most likely.

* * *

Work was as mundane as ever. I arrived home at around seven p.m., thinking that everything was back to normal. But when I got back to my room, I soon saw that this was not the case. I tried my key in the lock – I usually opened the door directly with the key, not wanting to knock in case Alanyo was sleeping – but the key no longer fit! Maria opened the door and I could see from her red eyes that she'd been crying.

"What's wrong?" I asked. "What's up with the lock, I can't get my key to work."

"We're being expulsed," she wailed. "Some maintenance guy came round and changed the lock. Look."

She showed me a letter indicating that we were effectively being kicked out for infringement of the rules; apparently the turning a blind eye to overnight visitors rule didn't stretch to little kids, especially ones that cried all night. Someone must have complained about the noise of a crying baby this weekend. We had until tomorrow midday to vacate the room. It was signed by the residence's female, battleaxe director, so there was no point in appealing. She was renowned for her strictness and suffered from a complete lack of empathy. I knew of another student who'd been expulsed just for having a rowdy party where a few bottles got thrown out of the window.

I glared at her angrily. "This is all your fault! You and that girning brat of yours. Where am I going to stay for the next two months? My summer job goes on until the end of September."

"We'll find a place, Sandy. Please! We can get a cheap hotel room for a few days until we find another place to stay."

"No, Maria, no! I think this is where we go our separate ways. You're taking your son and you're going back to your husband. You're going to apologize and I'm sure he'll take you back. I'm going to see if I can move in with a friend for my remaining time in Paris. You and me – it's over!" It was really time to step away. I was sure Henry would take me in if I asked nicely and I was discrete about staying there. Half the people staying here had their girlfriend, boyfriend or one or two mates staying over unofficially. As long as you weren't too noisy, as long as you didn't have a screaming wean, you were fine.

That night Alanyo cried a little before falling asleep around nine p.m. He then slept peacefully through the night – perhaps he knew he was going back to his real dad. He seemed contented enough anyway. It was Maria that did most of the crying that night. She was still crying and pleading with me when we went to bed around midnight. I was all set just to go to sleep, but she pulled me towards her. "Come on, Sandy, make love to me," she implored. "Be my man."

As always I didn't need much persuasion, and I made love to her with even more fervour than usual. I knew that this would probably be our last time together. As she reached orgasm, she began crying again, and I had to hold her, to soothe her with the only reassuring words I could muster under the circumstances. "You'll be all right, Maria. Don't worry. You and Alanyo will be fine." She eventually settled down and we drifted off to sleep for one final time in each other's arms.

In the morning I took the last of my things over to Henry's room. He'd accepted to let me stay and I'd already packed most of my stuff and taken it over to his before turning in with Maria the previous night.

I think Maria had finally resigned herself to the fact that it was over between us. She made one last desperate attempt at saving our relationship as I was leaving for work. "I love you, Sandy!" she said. "We can still be together. Come back to me in a year, once you've finished your studies." But the defeat was evident in her voice. Deep down, we both knew that this would be our final farewell.

"Take care, Maria," I said. Then I kissed her, ruffled Alanyo's hair and stepped away.

Chapter 10

Building a Marriage
on Rock(y) and Sand(y)

The Erasmus dream experience was back on track. I got a cheap inflatable mattress for Henry's room and settled in no problems. He was cool about everything.

"You did the right thing, bro," he reassured me. "It's okay to play around but you don't want to be a marriage breaker. Especially when there are kids involved. I take it they went back to the husband?"

"Yes," I replied. "He forgave her apparently. They've patched things up." Or so Gisella had told me. I'd forgiven her for getting me into such a mess to start with by telling Maria where I lived and taken up my casual sex relationship with her as before.

Then there was Rocky of course. I couldn't get enough of her – she was just fun to be around and so sexy. Any time I wanted to bring her over, Henry would oblige by leaving us his room while he went off to stay with Beverly. As the summer neared its end I felt myself falling in love with her.

The night before I headed back to Scotland I took her out for a meal. I decided to splash out on a nice restaurant to mark the occasion – Le 14 Juillet, one of Paris' best-kept secrets – hidden away in the 14th district. Over a sumptuous meal of giblet salad, rump steak with *gratin dauphinoise* and *crème brûlée* washed down with rich, red Bordeaux wine, we declared our undying love for each other.

"To us, Rocky," I said, lifting my wineglass in a toast. "I love you."

"I love you too, Sandy," she said chinking her glass against mine.

"I don't want to leave tomorrow. Can I put you in my suitcase and bring you to Scotland?"

She smiled. "I would like to come. Maybe I can come and visit you in Glasgow."

I knew this wasn't going to happen, since she didn't have French nationality, and her temporary student's *carte de sejour* didn't allow her to travel anywhere in Europe except France. She could apply for a visa, of course, but this would most likely be rejected, since she wouldn't be coming on some official student placement, but just to visit her boyfriend. I doubted I could afford to come and visit her either, not until I had found a job after my final year of studies.

"It would be good if you could come or if I could come back for a visit here. But even if we can't, I promise to get a job here after my studies and then we can be together. Maybe Schlumberger will take me on."

At least this was a possibility; my job had gone okay, even if it had been rather boring, and the bosses seemed pleased with the work I'd done.

"Oh, Sandy, my love, that would be great." She squeezed my hand tenderly across the table. "We're just meant to be together."

Later that night we savoured our lovemaking, like the fine wine we'd just drunk. I knew that I would soon be thirsting for her love and that it would be a long time before I could satiate my longing in her arms again.

* * *

After all the exquisite pleasures of that Erasmus year in Paris, it was back to 'auld claes and porridge' in Glasgow. Fourth year was very tough for me, missing Rocky so much, trying to get reacclimatised to Scotland, and, of course, getting back into my studies. The final year meant final exams and working on a complex lab project. I had to get my head down if I wanted to pass with a decent grade.

So I seriously toned down on the drinking and the partying. Womanising was almost non-existent; I was still thinking obsessively of Rocky, and anyway I was back to being just another Joe Bloggs, an average Scottish guy in Scotland, nothing special or foreign or exotic.

One night I did get back together with Janet, for a one-night fling, so to speak. I'd ventured back to the Todd one night, even though it was rather far from the place I was staying: a student flat at the west-end of Renfrew Street, not far from the Mackintosh School of Architecture. She was there with some of her nurse friends but I bought her a drink and persuaded her to come for a few more – just the two of us, in another couple of bars in the centre. Then, both a little drunk we headed back to my flat for sex. As I made love to her, I closed my eyes and imagined I was with Rocky.

She left me her phone number, but looked at me rather strangely as she left the next day, as if she knew I wasn't really 'with' her. I only called her back in a couple of weeks, one Friday night when I was feeling particularly horny, but she gave me the brush off saying she was going out with her girlfriends. I suggested another night but she was non-committal, so I left it at that.

Just that one night with her had left me feeling rather guilty. Rocky and I hadn't promised to be faithful or anything like that, a year was a long time after all, but nevertheless I still thought of her as my girlfriend. I phoned her every weekend and we wrote each other letters, declaring how much we missed each other and how we couldn't wait to see each other. As far as I knew she wasn't seeing anyone else.

That one night with Janet was my only act of infidelity. Naturally, I was tempted a few times throughout that final year to go for other women, especially Lizzie, from my course. I was in the same laboratory for my project as her, and we became good friends. She would sometimes come over to my flat and we would work on tutorials or discuss things on our projects. Even if she wasn't physically my type, I liked the softness of her voice and the way she looked into my eyes. I never tried anything with her though, partly because of Rocky, but also just because she was my friend and I didn't want to destroy that. Sometimes when I was with her, I would think about the convent janitor, Dave's advice – 'settle doon' wi' a nice Scottish lass', and feel like reaching out to touch her, but something would prevent me: the memories of Rocky, her enticing smile, her soft black skin... the call of the bongos.

I got through the year, passed my exams and obtained a 2.1 honours degree in Electronic Engineering. When Schlumberger offered me a job at their Montrouge site on the outskirts of Paris, I jumped at the chance.

* * *

Things were back on with Rocky! As luck would have it, she'd moved out of her strict Aunt Odette's house and in with her cool Aunty Claire. Claire lived with her partner, Zeus and their baby son, Timothée – in a big apartment in Montrouge, within walking distance of my new job. They kindly allowed me to come and stay with Rocky. So in October 1992, I excitedly headed back to France to start my new job and to be with my love, Rocky.

Rocky had started working as a part-time nurse, while continuing her studies, and after a couple of months we had enough to pay a deposit and rent a little flat of our own – also in Montrouge. And so we settled into domestic bliss: earning decent money, going out for meals or to the cinema or a show at the weekend, and of course great sex. We used protection of course; both in our early twenties, we just wanted to have fun for the time being. We did talk about having children, but agreed to put it off at least for three or four years.

Then there was the subject of marriage. The two of us living together 'in sin' was frowned upon by both of our families. Despite my Catholic upbringing, I wasn't too keen on getting married – it was all too final and definitive for my liking. I felt that I loved Rocky, we got on great, but would it last? How would I feel about her in five years, in ten years? Did we really have enough in common? Commitment – a scary word.

But the months turned into years, the pressure built up from our two families, and Rocky began dropping not so subtle hints.

"It's so beautiful here," she said while holidaying in the South of France one summer. "We could maybe come back here on our honeymoon."

"This would be a good place to have *our* wedding reception," she said at the wedding of one of her cousins.

Then about four years after I'd moved back, my hand was forced. Rocky's student resident permit had run out. She'd finished her studies and was now a qualified specialised midwifery nurse – *sage femme* – as it's called in France, which word for word translates to 'wise woman.' The French administration had refused her request for a new permit and she found herself in the vicious circle of *sans papiers*. Unable to find a job because she didn't have papers and unable to obtain papers because she didn't have a job. The solution was for us to get married. Being married to a European Union national meant you could benefit from the family resident permit, without necessarily having a job.

"Will you marry me, Rocky?" I popped the question in the romantic setting of our favourite French restaurant – Le 14 Juillet.

"Oh yes, Sandy," Rocky of course replied. We'd already been living together for almost four years and had chosen the engagement ring together previously that day, so the surprise effect was minimal.

We set a date for Saturday, 1st March 1997: mad March day, what else? We hastily made all the arrangements: booked the mayor's and the church and the reception venue, sent out invitations, and bought some swanky clothes – a white dress for Rocky and a kilt for me.

* * *

Our marriage took place – for better and for worse – on a cold, rainy morning in Montrouge. The omens were more 'worse' than 'better.'

The first phase was the mayor's office. I was on time, but Rocky, as is traditional for the bride, was late; not just ten or twenty minutes, but a full hour late. The mayor was threatening to cancel the whole thing, since there was another marriage in half an hour's time. She eventually showed up and the mayor rushed through the civil ceremony.

"I now pronounce you man and wife," he said at the end. Then after we'd kissed and the round of applause had died down, there was a quick signing of the register and he then hustled us out. "Please make you way towards the exit."

The old proverb *'Marry in haste, repent at leisure,'* came to mind.

We rushed off in a convoy of honking cars to the church, where we were also late. At least the priest was cool about it.

"Welcome, Sandy and Roquelle, and to all you families and friends gathered here on this happy occasion," he said at the beginning of the ceremony. It was strange hearing her called Roquelle; everyone else just called her Rocky. My parents were wryly amused by the combination of Sandy Beech and Rocky Coste – that at least lived up to their expectations in the humorous names department. They were less enamoured by the fact that she was a black African. The Beeches were mostly blue-eyed blondes and tended to marry blue-eyed blondes. It was an unwritten tradition, like the Sandy Beech naming tradition: marry a blue-eyed blonde, keep 'good' genes in the family. Even someone with brown hair was frowned upon. Someone from another race – well, that was just unthinkable. Lizzie, from my university course would have been right up their street.

"Ivory Coast? Where the hell's that? An African! Why can't you just marry a beautiful blonde like yer ma'?" had been Dad's initial reaction.

Then there was the fact that she was from a poor background, only moderately educated and currently unemployed. A specialist nurse wasn't fit for their intelligent engineer son.

"A nurse!" Mum had said. "You wouldn't marry a nurse in Scotland would you? Can't you find someone who's a bit more your social equal?"

Of course she'd also meant racial equal, but hadn't said it explicitly. But I'd stuck to my choice despite their objections.

So on my side there were my parents, putting on brave faces despite their serious reservations about the marriage; my elder sister and her husband; my younger brother and my younger sister, who were both single; three Scottish friends who'd managed to be persuaded to come to Paris for the weekend, with their girlfriends in tow; a couple of work colleagues, also single; and a couple of French friends I'd met in a pub, one single, the other accompanied by his Polish wife. Rocky's parents were unable to come from the Ivory Coast, but her extended family who lived in Paris were all present – sisters, uncles, aunties, cousins and their wives, partners, children, etc. – and a multitude of friends. The priest told people to just sit anywhere, but everyone fell into the traditional layout, so the church was black on the left side and white on the right.

There was organ music and singing and the reading of passages from the Bible. I read the first reading in English, from the Old Testament and Rocky read the second one in French, from the New Testament. We'd chosen the readings we liked – on the theme of love. Then it was the priest's turn and what did he choose as the gospel reading? The parable of the wise and foolish builders, a passage often used at weddings, but one which I would have forbidden him to use since it goes on about a 'wise man, who built his house on a rock 'versus' a foolish man, who built his house on the sand.' If he'd just read it in French no one would have batted an eyelid – rock was 'roc' in French but sand was 'sable'; he insisted, though, in reading it first in French and then in faltering English. I'm sure the guy did it on purpose, pausing and glancing ever so slightly at Rocky when he read the word 'rock' and at me when he read the word 'sand.' Bastard.

I was in a rather black mood by the end of the ceremony, not helped by the dark clouds and driving rain. But it was our big day after all so I kept smiling throughout, determined to remain upbeat and positive whatever else the day might throw at us. Quite a few more calamities as it happened.

The meal served by the caterers was quite good – grilled bass, accompanied by mashed potatoes and mixed vegetables, however once they'd dished out all the food and put bottles of wine on the table, they realised that they didn't have any corkscrews to uncork them! Rather embarrassingly, we had to get the DJ to ask over the speaker system if anyone had a corkscrew, so that we could open the wine. Thank God for Zeus. He came up to our table and handed a corkscrew directly to me. It was the type that folded up – the corkscrew hidden inside, covered by a plastic protection and a metal bottle opener.

"Ah thanks, Zeus!" I said. "Let me do the honours."

As I opened up the corkscrew, a cockroach crawled out from within and onto my hand.

"Oh my God!" I instinctively flinched and the insect landed right on Rocky's dress and started crawling over it.

She started screaming, until one of the caterers came over and flicked it off with a napkin and it scurried away into a crack in the floorboards.

The priest – who was sitting at the far end of our table – thought this was very amusing and was still chuckling when he tucked into the fish. He suddenly quietened down though and when I looked over, I could see he was turning red – he was choking on a fish bone. Charles – who was sitting beside him, began hitting him on the back, but to no effect. *'A foolish man, who built his house on the sand,' eh?* I thought to myself. *Let him choke!* He fell to his knees.

Charles looked at me, "Do something, Sandy!"

I eventually went over and performed the Heimlich manoeuvre on him and managed to dislodge the offending fish bone. He was a lot more subdued after that and left soon after the meal.

Then there was the wedding cake later on in the evening. The lights went down and the caterers brought it out, a magnificent white, four tier cake illuminated with sparklers attached to it. It looked beautiful, until they brought it over and put it on the table in front of us and I noticed that the top three tiers were all damaged on one side.

"What the hell happened?" I hissed at one of the caterers.

"Oh just a slight mishap out in the car park," he said nervously. "Don't worry, sir, we scraped off all the pieces with dirt on them. We can take the photos from the other side."

Seriously! I glared at him, but said nothing and went to cut a piece of the cake – from the bottom tier. That was when I caught fire – must have been a spark from one of the fireworks.

"Ah! Sandy, look! Your jacket!" screamed Rocky.

I hastily ripped it off and doused it with a bottle of water; the lower right-hand side was all singed.

Still, we were all determined to not let such little accidents spoil the evening and dived wholeheartedly into the dancing. The DJ alternated African World music with tunes from a Scottish country dancing CD I'd handed him. The latter went down well with the Scots and Ivoirians alike, until Tim, my sister's husband, got a bit carried away on the burling of the Strip the Willow dance. He and some other guy, one of Rocky's friends, were spinning round and round, when suddenly Tim slipped on the polished wooden floor, went careering into a table and hurt his leg. It was so bad that we had to phone for an ambulance and he was carted off to hospital; broken leg it turned out.

That was our marriage: dark clouds, insects, choking priests, spoilt cake, fire, and broken bones; not quite the seven plagues, but not far off.

Chapter 11

Wedded Bliss

The honeymoon at least went well. We rented a quiet cottage by the sea in Corsica – the nearest you can get to a paradisiacal island in France. We made love by the cottage's wood fire, listening to the crackling flames and the waves breaking on the beach.

I even ventured out for a swim in those cold, March, Mediterranean waters. There was the initial excitement and shock as you plunged in, followed by swimming a few strokes and letting your body warm up a little and adjust to the cold, then after a while you could float on your back and feel the waves lapping against you. Not a good idea to stay in too long, though.

Rocky didn't do anything more than paddle.

"Are you mad!" she exclaimed when she felt how cold the water was on her feet.

"No, just Scottish," I replied. "Come on in for a swim. It's great – refreshing!"

"The water's glacial! No way!"

I came back onto the beach after a while and gave her a hug.

"Ah, you're all cold!" Rocky cried, but she returned my embrace – let me warm my cold, white skin against her warm, black flesh. Ebony and ivory, except, well, she was both ebony and ivory: ebony because of her black skin and ivory since she came from the Ivory Coast. And what was I?

"What are the beaches like in your country?" I asked her.

"Beautiful. White sand, coconut trees and a lot warmer than here. You'll see when we go and visit."

"That would be nice."

"As soon as I get my French papers sorted out, we can go and visit my family."

"Okay, cool. We can also go for a visit to my country, Scotland."

"Okay, Sandy, but let's go in the summer, eh? I've heard it's bitterly cold in winter."

"You've heard right, but I'll be there to keep you warm."

"Ooh!" She squeezed my hand. "I love you, Sandy."

"I love you too, Rocky"

* * *

It took over a year to get her papers sorted. French bureaucracy made Kafka's 'The Trial' look like a simple administrative procedure. Each time you had to queue for hours, just to be seen by some crusty old relic, who would eye you with suspicion, review your completed application forms and accompanying documents before declaring that some other document (never mentioned in any of the administration instructions for applicants) was required – your grandparents' birth certificates for example.

When they finally accepted our application, several months went by and then they sent some inspector to our house to check us out, make sure it wasn't a *mariage blanc*, a marriage just for the sake of obtaining French papers. The guy they sent was Métis, mixed white and black, maybe even a little Asian, dressed in khakis with an African style shirt and what looked like an Australian rancher's hat. Was he really a mix of several different races and cultures or was it just that he took his job so seriously that he'd adopted the styles and traditions of a whole bunch of people, all the better to suss them out? Or perhaps it was to create a connection by means of common culture, in order to lull you into a false sense of security, so that you would reveal all sorts of stuff to this guy who was African, European, Asian… just like you.

Anyway I was immediately wary of his friendly demeanour; it was obvious that he'd 'turned his jacket' so many times, he didn't know where he was really from, and who or what he was loyal too. Rocky naively seemed to warm to him, just because he claimed his grandmother was Ivoirian. I was thinking, *Yes, and I bet you turned her in to immigration for deportation back there, in exchange for some step up in your organisation's hierarchy.*

When I told him I was Scottish, I was half expecting him to stake some claim on some great-grandmother from Islay, but all he said was, "Ah, beautiful country. I've been there salmon fishing."

Such a stereotype. I felt like calling his bluff on this. *Oh really, on which river? At what period of the year?* But I held my tongue, remembering that it was us that were supposed to be convincing him of our integrity and not vice versa.

He questioned us on how we'd met, our jobs, our families, did we want to have children together, did we want to settle in France... and so on – all with that annoying insincere smile on his face. By the end of his visit I felt like punching him right in the mouth, just to quickly make that smile disappear. But at last he left, prattling on about African drums and malt whisky.

Apparently, we'd been believable enough – ours was a marriage of love and not of convenience – and about a month later Rocky received the letter to go and pick up her papers. She collected the elusive *carte de sejour* on a Friday and we organised a little party on the Saturday at our flat, to celebrate. We invited Claire, Zeus, and their little son, Timothée, and Rocky's friend Katy. Claire brought some *tchep*, which is a Senegalese speciality, not Ivoirian, consisting of round rice and fish cooked in a red sauce with spices. It tastes a bit like haggis.

So we had a delicious meal washed down with a mixture of beer, wine and whisky. Katy had even brought a bottle of champagne, which we popped open with the apple tart dessert.

"So are you going to hold onto this guy, now that you've got your papers?" joked Zeus, pointing at me.

"Of course," replied Rocky. "He's my Rock."

"Well actually you're the Rock and I'm the Sand, remember?" I said.

Claire used this as a cue to start chanting, "Rocky and Sandy! Rocky and Sandy!" And the others joined in.

It seemed at that moment that our couple was unstoppable, that the whole world belonged to us. We'd conquered French immigration bureaucracy, we could do anything – work on decent jobs for decent money, go travelling and maybe start having a family.

* * *

With her ten year *carte de sejour* now in her pocket, Rocky soon found a good well-paid job as a *sage femme* in a big hospital in Kremlin Bicetre – another close suburb of Paris. I continued with Schlumberger and for the next few years we lived the good life: going out most weekends to restaurants, cinemas, concerts, parties; and going on holidays in France, Spain and Germany. The UK was a bit trickier, since it was not part of the Schengen agreement and Rocky still needed a visa to go there, but we did manage to visit at least once a year – applying for a visa a good three months in advance. We talked about visiting the Ivory Coast, but put it off, Rocky saying we needed to save up to buy presents for her family, not to mention the plane tickets.

We celebrated the new millennium on the Champs Elysées with Claire, her new guy Sarafin – her marriage with Zeus was as good as over, and a few other friends and workmates. There were fireworks and champagne and singing and dancing and kissing; we all felt elated, full of hope for the future. Later that night, walking back, just the two of us, from the metro to our house, we brought up the subject of kids.

"Let's have a baby, Rocky!" I proposed. "A little new

millennium baby!"

"Yes, let's do it, this year. I love children. I want to have your child so much."

"You'd make a great mum."

"Sure you're ready to be a dad?"

"Of course. We've been married almost four years. Let's do it!"

"Okay – a cute little Sandy-Rocky Métis."

That night we made love thinking about the baby. Of course she was still on the pill, so she wasn't about to become pregnant there and then, but after that night she went off the pill and we seriously went about trying to start a family.

Trying. At first having sex three or four times a week as usual; still no pregnancy after six months. Her periods came every month, regular as clockwork. Then sex more or less every night for the following six months. Then doctor's consultations – we were both fine and fertile apparently; just keep at it, they said. They showed us how to calculate on a calendar the best time to 'do it' – ten days after the beginning of her period. More months passed. Rocky lost her job – maternity ward cuts apparently, and started to get a bit depressed. She'd mope around the house, watching trashy sitcoms and eating junk food: chocolate, popcorn, crisps and this strange chalky substance, which she got in one of the African boutiques she frequented in the Château Rouge district of Paris. Sometimes she'd blame herself; other times me.

"Why can't you get me pregnant?" she berated me. "You're useless."

"Come on, Rocky. We need to just keep on trying. Don't give up hope."

The sex was still good of course, but after a while it lost some of its excitement – we were just doing it mechanically. For the baby. Plus, Rocky started putting on weight, with all the crap she was eating. I began to lose my desire for her, due to her chubbiness and her moodiness. So after a while we made love less and less. By early 2002, our sex life was non-existent – even when I did feel like it, she would turn her back and claim a headache or period pains.

In May 2002, I had to book my holidays for the summer. In France you could easily get three or four weeks off during the summer, if you had accumulated enough holiday leave.

I proposed a trip to see my family in Scotland. Rocky had other ideas.

"Don't you think it's about time we went to *my* country?" she said. "Please, Sandy! You'll love it. I'll take you to see the rest of my family. You can chill out in the village, and we can go to the beaches – they're beautiful, you'll see."

I thought about this. The subject of visiting the Ivory Coast hadn't come up for a while. We had enough saved up to be able to afford the trip and bring presents for her family. Maybe this visit was just what we needed to get our marriage back on track. Who knew, perhaps a change of scenery would even help us conceive the baby we'd been trying so hard for.

"Okay, Rocky. Let's do it. Let's book it!"

She threw herself into my arms. It was the happiest I'd seen her for a long time.

I managed to obtain a full four weeks off work for the trip. We booked it from Saturday, 24th of August to Saturday, 21st of September. The prices were a bit cheaper, since this was almost at the end of the season. I asked Rocky about booking hotels, but she said not to worry about that, we'd mostly be staying with her family, and that we'd get a hotel no problem in Abidjan, for a few nights at the start of the trip and a few nights on the way back. We each packed a case and Rocky added two more cases full of presents – clothes, handbags, some jewellery and little souvenirs of Paris.

The big day arrived. We humped our luggage into a taxi and set off for a Swiss Air flight – via Zurich – to Abidjan, Ivory Coast.

Part IV

Chapter 12

Abidjan

Travelling by plane to the Ivory Coast is a fairly luxurious experience. Swiss Air provided us with individual TV screens, headphones, music, and lots of food and drink to keep us going on the six hour flight from Zurich to Abidjan. Flying into Abidjan we could see the coconut and palm trees lining the lagoons and a skyline of skyscrapers – a kind of African New York. We arrived just as the sun was setting, and it was breathtakingly beautiful.

Abidjan is in fact similar to the Big Apple, in that it is built on several portions of land – islands, peninsulas, etc. – divided by a complex system of lagoons and waterways and split into different districts or boroughs. It has a central business district called Le Plateau, similar to Manhattan. The well to do district of Cocody lies to the east. To the south are the popular districts of Treichville, Marcory and the industrial Koumassi. To the west, across the Bay of Banco, are the districts of Attécoubé and Yopougon. To the north there is the Forest of Banco and districts of Adjamé and Abobo. Finally, to the far south lies the tenth borough of Port-Bouët, which houses the airport, a refinery and beaches. The best beaches, though, are about thirty kilometres to the south east, in Grand Bassam, just like the Long Island Beaches beside New York.

Once we hit the ground though, the luxury and the beauty were rapidly replaced with African reality. As soon as we got off the plane, we could see porters lazing around on top of the carousels and on boxes and crates. Then once we got into the airport building, there were more porters and other dodgy looking geezers – taxi-drivers, hotel representatives and tour-guides – waiting on the other side of passport control, all prepared to 'welcome us' and help us with our luggage. A throng of would-be helpers and guides dived on top of us and started talking a lot of bullshit, trying to get us to accept their 'services,' and no doubt hoping to squeeze as much money out of us as possible. We were supposed to be meeting Frank, one of Rocky's cousins, but there was no sign of him, so we reluctantly accepted the help of the meekest looking porter, if only to get rid of the rest of the horde.

There were signs saying 'Offical Porters Fee 500 FCFA' – roughly five French francs. Our guy immediately asked for ten times this. I pointed to the signs. "Isn't it supposed to just be a fixed fee of five hundred francs CFA?"

"Trust me," he replied. "You need to pay me a bit more, so I can give some to customs to get though, no problems."

In Abidjan, the customs also searched your bags on arrival and could apparently claim taxes if they thought you were bringing in merchandise to be sold: Rocky's two big cases of presents! We'd already had to cough up excess luggage fees to Swiss Air.

"Come on, Sandy," piped in Rocky. "Just pay him."

We settled on four thousand francs CFA; we'd obtained some of the currency from Rocky's relatives in Paris. The customs officer opened up our cases, asked a few questions, gave a desultory rifle through our stuff then nodded us through. I hadn't noticed the porter giving him any of the money. I suspected that he'd just kept all the money for himself, but didn't say anything, giving him the benefit of the doubt that the bribe was indeed passed on to the customs officer, but so subtly as to be totally unnoticeable.

We at last found Rocky's cousin, Frank, outside in the car park, chatting up some French girl tourists. The porter managed to pack all the cases into Frank's car and then we headed to the district of Marcoury – to his mum's house, Rocky's Aunt Elia. On the road there, I took in my first views of daily life in the Ivory Coast. Women walked by the roadside with loads of firewood or big plastic water-containers on their heads. Men carried live chickens, holding them upside down by their ankles. Little kids came up to our car at traffic lights to sell us water or chewing gum or *lotus* – little packets of paper handkerchiefs.

We arrived at Elia's place, a small concrete house with a corrugated tin roof, around five p.m. We had some tea and a chat, and Rocky handed over a few presents from one of her big cases. There wasn't enough space for us to stay there, so Frank drove us to a nearby hotel called Hotel Hamanieh. It was an all-inclusive dinner, bed and breakfast deal, probably aimed at businessmen on a budget. The place was clean – an army of cleaning staff saw to that, scouring the place from top to bottom every morning. There was an armed security guard out front 24 hours a day. All in all, the place was not too bad. Despite all its good points, we decided to leave after a couple of nights, since we found the food very bland, and since we thought we'd spend a lot less by just paying for a hotel and eating out separately.

We left this clean, comfortable, reputable establishment for a hotel with no name – recommended by Rocky's cousin, Frank, whom I'd immediately clocked as something of a playboy. This was confirmed by the new 'hotel,' which we soon found out was a seedy *hôtel de passe*: a place where men could take prostitutes or illicit lovers to pass the night in secrecy, *en toute discrétion, ni vu ni connu* – as they say in French. It had little private covered drive-in entrances to each room, horizontal mirrors beside each bed, stain-covered walls, and smelly sheets, which we had to hassle reception to change. The only thing on the TV was some 24 hour porn channel.

Still it was dirt cheap and a short walk away from a great little *maquis* – restaurants where you could get delicious barbecued fish, accompanied with rice and spicy sauce, washed down with a few bottles of beer, all for about five hundred francs CFA.

To get from the hotel to the little district with the restaurants, you had to walk through a shanty town, crossing dusty courtyards where gangs of children played alongside clucking chickens and stray cats and dogs. After a ten-minute walk you arrived in the heart of Treichville, with shops of all varieties, telephone booths, car repair places, tailors using foot-driven sewing machines and woodcarving workshops. You could buy almost anything, product or service, in this neighbourhood. Rocky got me a couple of shirts and a suit made to measure at one of the tailors; you just chose the material, gave them your measurements and in a couple of days you could pick up great quality, perfectly fitting clothes for a fraction of the price you'd pay in Europe for the *prêt-à-porter* variety.

* * *

Apart from hanging around in Treichville, we also made a few outings during those first days of our stay – to Le Plateau and to Grand Bassam. To get to Le Plateau we just flagged down a taxi – easily identifiable by their orange colour. Taxis in Abidjan were so ubiquitous that you didn't have any trouble finding one, in fact, often they found you. They'd see you walking along and drive up beside you tooting their horns and gesturing at you. We found this pretty bizarre. Let's face it, when you're looking for a taxi, you look, see one, and flag one down. You don't need some guy tooting at you, so you can say to yourself, *Oh yeah come to think of it I do feel like getting a taxi, thanks very much for alerting me to your presence.* Most of the taxis in Abidjan have meters, although it is quite usual to negotiate a fixed price with the driver as soon as you set off. I don't know the reason for this. Maybe it's because there are so many taxis that the drivers are willing to take slightly less than the meter-price, just so that they will get the fare, or to avoid fights at the end of the journey if there is some disagreement over the fare. So like most things in the Ivory Coast, taxi fares are to be haggled over. When you stick to using the meter, you also have to be careful that they don't put you on tariff two – the night-time tariff, which is only supposed to be used after midnight.

On day three, we hit Le Plateau. We spent two hours in the morning waiting in a queue at the bank, just to withdraw some money; electronic distributors were practically non-existent back then, and the few that did exist didn't accept our visa card. We had lunch in a western-style fast food joint, then visited the modern Saint Paul's Cathedral – another taxi-trip to the north of Le Plateau. There was an unofficial guide who showed us around, pointing out the different saints depicted in the stained glass windows and spouting out other facts and figures. Rocky elbowed me in the ribs at the end of his tour, to remind me to give him a tip.

After visiting the Cathedral, we decided just to head back to Treichville, so we hopped into the back of a taxi at the front of a taxi-queue. We gave the driver the address of our hotel in Treichville, but he just looked at us for a few seconds in his rear-view mirror then hissed, "Get out!"

I was starting to get used to the severe rudeness of the taxi-drivers, but this was just over the top.

"What's the problem?" I asked.

He turned around in his seat, a strange look of disgust on his face and shouted angrily, "I'm not taking you! I'm not going there! Get out!" He was so worked up his hands were trembling and he was gripping what looked like a small crucifix, on a chain round his neck.

It was evident there was no point in trying to reason with him any longer, so we just got out without further discussion, and got in the next cab in the queue, who took us there no problem.

"What was wrong with that guy?" I asked Rocky. "Why did he refuse to take us?"

"Who knows," she replied, apparently unperturbed. "You know racism exists here, too. Maybe he just can't stand the thought of a white guy with a black girl."

That seemed a rather unlikely explanation to me. Why was he gripping the crucifix? But I left it at that.

On day four we took a different type of taxi – a *taxi-collectif* (shared taxi) – to Grand Bassam. Where a normal taxi fare would be rather expensive, for a journey of about 30 km in this case, the taxi-collectif was the cheap option. These are basically big estate or station wagon cars – usually Peugeot 505s – with two back rows of passenger seats so that they can carry up to ten people: two in the front plus four in each of the back seats.

We got the taxi-collectif early that morning, at a pickup point on the main road towards Grand Bassam. It took quite a long time, over an hour, due to all the dropping people off and picking new people up, and was rather squashed. At times there were ten adults, plus a few more children or small people squeezed in, not to mention baggage, chickens, etc. So I was glad when we finally got to our destination and could stretch our legs and feel the cool sea breeze. The beaches were just a twenty-minute walk from the town centre, where the taxi-collectif had dropped us. There was some activity on the way, in the form of little artisan stalls selling a wide variety of painted tissues, table-cloths, tam-tam drums, wooden sculptures, even chairs, cupboards and beds made from wood and bamboo. However, when we got to the beach itself, the place was practically deserted. The waves were massive, but I ventured in for a swim. It was great to get into that refreshing water, then laze after on the white sands of the beach, in the shade of a coconut tree.

"This is the life, eh, Rocky?" I said.

She wasn't that strong a swimmer, and the currents were very strong – especially dangerous for someone like her, so she'd just rolled up her trousers and had a paddle on the shore, despite me taunting her to stop being a chicken and come in for a swim. Was she really that frightened of the currents, or just of stripping down to a swimsuit and letting me see how fat she'd become?

Yes," she agreed. "I told you you'd love it here."

"Oh look," she continued. "There's someone selling fresh coconuts. Let's get some – they're delicious."

A woman with a big basin of coconuts on her head came over and we bought two. She deftly cut off the top with a machete and even more skilfully chipped off a bit of the shell to use as a spoon. They were indeed delicious, the juice cool and tasty, and the flesh, which you scooped out with the little shell-spoon, so soft and sweet; a world away from the hard, dried variety which you sometimes get in Europe.

After we'd finished eating them, I kissed Rocky long and hard and felt myself aroused for the first time in ages.

"It's been a while, Rocky. Let's make love, as soon as we get back to the hotel," I suggested.

She looked down at my bulging Bermuda trunks and smiled, "Okay, Sandy."

Her depression seemed to be vanishing under the Ivoirian sun.

We got lunch – *aloko* (fried plantain bananas) and sardines wrapped in banana leaves, then had a wander round the little market stalls and bought some painted tissues, tie-dye t-shirts, masks, and other small wooden sculptures as souvenirs – bargaining like mad to get a half decent price.

Late afternoon, we got another taxi-collectif back to the hotel. I began fondling her as soon as we got in the door.

"Go and have a shower first, Sandy," Rocky suggested. "Get the salt off your skin."

My skin *was* feeling a bit itchy after the swim in the salt water; there were no showers there, apart from on the private beaches belonging to a couple of luxury hotels, and we hadn't brought enough water to rinse off with. "Okay, Rocky. I'll just be a few minutes."

"Switch on the porn channel if you like, to get in the mood." I winked at her.

She just rolled her eyes and laughed.

When I was in the shower though, I heard her switching on the TV and the moans of the porn-actors. At one point I thought I heard the phone ring, and Rocky talking to someone, but I couldn't make out what she was saying with the noise of the TV and the running water. After my shower I quickly dried myself off and just tied the towel round my waist before heading back into the bedroom, but when I got there, Rocky had left, leaving a hastily scribbled note:

Sorry, Sandy, I have to go and see my Aunt Béatrice urgently. If I'm not back by dinner time, just go to one of the maquis for a meal and I'll meet you back here at the hotel.
Love you, Rocky

She'd drawn a little love heart with an arrow through it, at the end of the note.

Love you. Strange way of showing it, dashing off when we're just about to make love. What could be so urgent?

I switched off the porn, lay on the bed and read some of a horror novel I'd brought for the trip, but couldn't really concentrate. What the hell was Rocky doing, leaving me alone like this? The mosquitoes were driving me mad too. I'd killed a few with a rolled up newspaper, adding to the multitude of smears on the walls, but more kept on coming – there seemed to be an endless supply of them.

After a couple of hours, around 6.15 p.m., I got fed up, and headed out to the thriving hub of Treichville. The sun was just setting and a lot of people were knocking off work. Suited business men scurried off home, or to bars more likely. Manual workers, tired and dusty, stopped for a drink of water or fruit juice, sold in little plastic sachets which you bit the corner off before sucking out the liquid, and then most people threw them on the ground - the whole place was littered with them. The most striking were the mechanics, crawling out from ancient carcasses of cars and dismantled motors, their ragged, oil-blackened clothes just seemed to merge with their oil-covered legs and arms. I wandered round the busy streets for a while, just taking in all the eclectic activity of that warm summer's night: children sold drinks, eggs and nuts, again in little sachets or more inventively, old coke or whisky bottles; men chinked glasses or bottles of beer together at bars; women sold fruit or rice and sauce served up from massive cauldrons; boys offered to clean your shoes; and a couple of women – probably prostitutes – proposed that I accompany them for a drink.

I eventually got a bit hungry, so I headed to one of the maquis and ordered a plate of braised fish with the spicy sauce and rice, plus a nice big cool bottle of beer. I listened in to the conversation at an adjoining table – men solving the world's problems over a few drinks, as they do in bars throughout the world. I got a bit lost when they started taking about Ivoirian politics, something about some guy called Outtara not being allowed to stand for president because his father was Burkinabé – from the neighbouring country of Burkina Faso.

After drinking three or four more beers, I left the maquis and headed back towards the hotel. It was around midnight, but the streets were still buzzing at that time, even on a Tuesday night. However, as I got nearer to the hotel it got quieter and quieter. By the time I was crossing one of the last dusty courtyards before the hotel, it was eerily quiet, not even the bleating of a goat, and quite dark, just the odd light in a window to break the blackness.

Suddenly I heard a ferocious growling. I looked over to the source of the sound – a nearby clump of bushes, and could see the glowing eyes of some animal. It came out of hiding; a big, black dog – a mongrel of unidentifiable parentage. It was baring its teeth and growling even louder, and there was something rather disturbing about the look in those glowing eyes. I broke into a run, but the beast lunged at my left leg and bit in hard! I could feel the teeth going in like a hundred little daggers. I tried to shake the dog off, kicking it with my right foot and even hitting it with my hands, but it continued biting into the lower calf muscle of my left leg. The pain was excruciating and I could see drops of blood falling off into the dust.

I cried out, "Help! Get this thing off me!"

Then someone appeared from nowhere and swung a big wooden stick at the dog. I looked up – it was Rocky; she'd shown up at last. The dog relaxed it's jaws slightly, which allowed me to extract my leg. Rocky hit the dog again and it backed off, still snarling – it's teeth red with my blood.

Rocky pressed a clean paper handkerchief to my wound. "Hold it with your hand," she said.

Then we walked quickly back to the hotel. She was still wielding the stick in case the dog tried to attack again. I was trembling uncontrollably with shock and I kept looking fearfully over my shoulder to make sure the dog wasn't there. Once inside our room, she fished out some antiseptic ointment from our first aid kit, cleaned the wound, then took out a syringe filled with some fluid and plunged it into the skin just beside the wound before I could say anything.

"Oww! What's that?" I cried.

"Rabies shot, just in case," she replied calmly, bandaging up the wound.

Really reassuring! I thought, slowly coming out of my shock. "Shouldn't we go to the hospital to get it checked out properly? Maybe I need a tetanus shot as well. They could also put a better dressing on it."

"You'll be fine – it doesn't look that bad," she replied. "I'm a nurse remember. That dressing I've just done is as professional as anything you'll get at a hospital. Plus, you had a tetanus jab just before we came here, remember?"

That was true. It had been part of the series of injections I'd had, along with the malaria tablets. I'd need all the protection I could get in this place. The mosquitoes in the room were more frenzied than ever, no doubt attracted by the smell of fresh blood from my wounded leg.

"Tomorrow, we're leaving this fleapit," I said firmly. "Where the hell have you been anyway? Who's this Aunt Béatrice?"

"Don't worry. It's all planned. We're leaving tomorrow, to see my family in Guédéyo. I had to see Béatrice urgently about a family matter."

"So how are we getting there?"

"We'll catch a bus to Soubré, then a baca from there to the village."

"What the heck's a baca?"

"It's just a mini-bus; they take people from the larger towns out to smaller villages. Don't worry, Sandy, it'll be fine."

"Okay, if you say so. So when do we have to leave?"

"We'll get a taxi tomorrow morning around 8 a.m. to the bus station in Adjamé."

* * *

Adjamé – what a nightmare! Rubbish strewn all over the place, human / animal faeces, large puddles of stagnant water, children urinating, and amongst all this squalor people selling stuff every-where: at market stalls, small shops or cabins, in bowls on people's heads or just strewn out on the ground – fruit, vegetables and all sorts of other products – amongst the filth. Arriving by taxi via the relatively clean district of Le Plateau, the disgusting smell hit us as we approached the district of Adjamé. It would remain impregnated on our hair and clothes even once we'd left later by bus.

The crowds became impenetrable at one point and the taxi suddenly came to a halt. A nimble young lad – he must have been only about fourteen – immediately appeared at our window. "Where are you going?" he asked. He was barefoot, dressed in ragged shorts and t-shirt, and had very athletic legs for his age. I was about to find out why.

I let Rocky do the talking. "Adjamé bus station," she replied.

"Yes, but there are several bus stations here," said the lad. "What's your final destination? San Pedro? Yamoussoukro?"

"Guédéyo, near Soubré."

"Okay, just follow me."

He ran on in front of the vehicle, guiding the driver through various obstacles, shouting at people to get out of the way, helping up old women who were selling their wares, and giving the occasional kick to any sheep or goats that were blocking our path.

We eventually made it through the chaos to our 'bus station.' It was just a stall selling tickets, a few chairs for people to sit and wait on, and a bit of space for the buses to park. We paid our young guide a couple of hundred francs, and then he ran off, presumably for his next customers. We bought two tickets at the stall, but our bus didn't leave for another hour, so we had a little wander round some of the stalls, adding all our cases and bags to a big pile of other passengers' luggage by the ticket office. Rocky assured me they'd be safe, paradoxically adding that we should remove all jewellery, and watch out for our belongings at all times as we wandered around; that people had had earrings ripped off their ears, necklaces snatched off their necks, or even their wrists broken as someone wrestled off their watch. I stashed my watch, not exactly a Rolex, in my little blue rucksack, where I carried valuables like passports and travel documents, and wore it on my front. To be fair though, the place was filthy and smelly but it didn't feel dangerous, at least not then, in broad daylight. I'm sure night-time would be a different kettle of fish.

Three young lads, about the same age as the 'runner' tagged along with us. I suppose you could describe them as being aggressively friendly.

"What would you like to buy – masks, clothes, fruit? What would you like to visit, the mosque, the church… go to a bar?"

They bombarded us with questions and proposals.

We don't need anything really, we're just killing time, I felt like saying.

"Where can we get a packet of biscuits?" Rocky asked, making up something just to keep them happy, so they could show us something and then we could give them a tip.

From what I could see, most of the little stalls and shops sold biscuits, but they led us through the maze of little boutiques to a slightly bigger shop, which did indeed have a good selection of biscuits, along with practically everything else under the sun – radios, gas cookers, dried fish, alcohol, toothbrushes. We got a couple of packets of Prince biscuits.

"What else do you need?" they pressed us. "How about going to see some beautiful traditional masks?"

"Er, is there a toilet somewhere?" I asked. It was a good idea to take a piss before the journey, not knowing how long we'd be cooped up in the bus before reaching Soubré or stopping for a break.

This seemed to stump them. They muttered away in some local language amongst themselves, and then the ringleader smiled and said simply, "Follow us!"

They led us to a building which was very clean looking, especially for Adjamé.

Men were washing their hands and faces outside, with water poured from little kettles. I didn't realise this at the time but they were Muslims performing their ritual ablutions. It was just beside our bus station, so this was the ideal time to tip them and say our goodbyes.

"Thanks a lot, guys!" I gave two hundred francs CFA to the ringleader, but Rocky indicated the other two with her eyes, so I had to give two hundred each to them as well.

I went inside and a young guy, sitting on a carpet greeted me, "As-salaam Alaikum."

I looked around – there was a big open area inside, strewn

with carpets. "Hello. What is this place?" I asked.

"It's a mosque, brother. Welcome," the young man replied, smiling.

"Ah. I'm not actually a Muslim. I'm Catholic."

"We're all brothers, my friend. God will guide you."

Right now I just wanted to be guided to the toilet. "Can you show me where the toilet is please?"

The guy kept smiling, unfazed. "Pipi?"

"Eh, yeah."

"Just go round the back." He indicated a door which was slightly ajar.

I headed out the door and surprisingly, there was a large open area of wasteland, mostly just dusty earth with a few weeds growing. The land sloped gently down to some houses about four hundred meters away. I took a piss up against the windowless wall, went back through the mosque, thanked the guy who'd welcomed me, and then we headed to our bus, which would be leaving shortly.

Our bus was a medium sized coach, which looked reasonably roadworthy. When we got there, there was a lot of shouting and commotion as people got on board and handed their cases and big bags to be stashed up on a large roof rack on top of the bus. The bus tickets to Soubré had only cost five hundred francs CFA each, but we found out that there was a bit of a scam because they charged you extra for each bag that you brought on. We ended up paying five hundred francs CFA for each of our four cases. The bus was supposed to leave at ten a.m. officially, but with all the bargaining everyone wasn't on board until eleven and then we waited around for another half an hour for some reason, while people moaned more and more vociferously at the drivers.

"Why aren't we leaving?"

"What are you bandits waiting for?"

"We've forked out our money; can we get on the road now?"

Eventually, at eleven thirty, we were off. One guy drove and he had two helpers to get luggage down when people wanted to get off. Once we were out of Abidjan the roads were fairly smooth, wide motorways. The trip was long, about six hours in all, but fairly uneventful. The bus made a few official stops in places like Lakota and Gagnoa, and a couple of stops at service stations, to fill up on fuel and let people out to go to the toilet or stretch their legs for a few minutes. At each of these stops, whether it be town, village or garage, a bunch of young children, typically girls aged ten or so, would come over to the bus windows, selling bags of cool water, peanuts, baked bananas, sweet bananas, sweet bread, cans of coke and the ever-present 'Lotus': small plastic bags of paper handkerchiefs. They also sometimes provided sandwiches, filled with meat and onions, wrapped in a bit of paper ripped from an old sack or attiéké (cooked ground manioc) and fish, wrapped in a big leaf. All this stuff they carried in big bowls on top of their heads. For a few hundred francs CFA, we were kept well fed throughout the long journey; it also felt good to be contributing in some small way to the livelihoods of the local people in these villages. Getting change though was a bit of a problem. We didn't have many coins or small-denomination notes, but mostly 1000, 5000 and 10 000 francs CFA bills from the bank, so the girls would usually work something out such as going off to a shop to exchange these big bills for smaller notes and coins. In some cases we just let them keep the change.

The journey was made longer by the unofficial stops, people wanting to be let out at various places on the way which weren't part of the official stops. Mostly the drivers complied, after a bit of grumbling and heated argument. But they made one young lad – who apparently didn't have any luggage to reclaim from up top – jump off from the moving bus. They slowed down to maybe ten kilometres per hour but even still the poor kid went flying as he jumped out the front door and the whole bus burst out laughing.

The boy scowled back at the amused drivers and passengers, but I could see him getting up and dusting himself off as the bus picked up speed again. Thankfully he hadn't broken anything, not that the maverick bus drivers could have cared a jot.

Six hours later we arrived in Soubré, a medium sized town, with a big market place and bus station, apparently the transport hub of the region. Thankfully it was a lot more salubrious than Adjamé. We got all of our luggage off and checked when the next bus to Rocky's home village of Guédéyo was. In an hour's time apparently, so we dumped our luggage in the big pile beside the ticket office – apparently this is the done thing everywhere in the Ivory Coast, and went for a quick wander round the market.

At six fifteen p.m. we showed up for the bus, and I found out what a baca really meant: a rust-covered old wreck, with wires hanging out beneath the steering wheel, patched up seats and broken windows replaced with thin slices of wood. For the bacas, you just paid as you got on – a set price according to your destination, so no bargaining, extra for bags, etc. That meant there was a lot less hanging around and the baca left more or less on time. The bus was full, people crammed in four or five to a row in four rows of seats.

We were told it was 40 km and so expected to arrive in forty-five minutes or so. It ended up taking about two and a half hours! This was due to the state of the roads, which were really just hole ridden dirt tracks. The holes and long ridges are created due to the rain forming streamlets or puddles which erode or redistribute the dust / mud making up the road. Hence the journey was rather slow and bumpy. During the journey, seats were liberated as people got off at various points; although other people also got on. I was a bit nervous about the state of the bus, that it might break down or one of our bags fall off the roof, but the guys running the baca had it down to a fine art. There was a driver and a helper who sat on a little wooden block at the back exit. They jabbered away to each other in a language I couldn't understand, but which Rocky informed me was Dyula – the vehicular language largely used in the Ivory Coast, so that people of different ethnicities with different native languages can communicate with each other. Apparently, there are seventy-eight different languages spoken in the country! The helper's block of wood doubled as a brake, the hand brake didn't appear to work, and at each stop the helper would get out and stick the block of wood behind or in front of one of the wheels. He'd also take fares and help people get their baggage on and off the roof. All in all it was quite efficient; credit had to be given to the mechanics that had kept the rust-bucket going so long and to the guys running the bus, for their system of driving passengers around in it so proficiently, despite all its deficiencies.

The sun had already set when we left Soubré and by the time we arrived in Guédéyo, it was pitch black.

Chapter 13

Guédéyo (Also Known as Ottawa)

Arriving in darkness, and due to the fact that she hadn't been there for years, Rocky didn't recognise her village at first; she had to check with a woman getting off that this was definitely Guédéyo. Rocky's father's house was right beside where the baca stopped. There were no streetlights, but the obscurity was broken by a mixture of torches and paraffin-lamps.

Rocky's father and mother, André and Betty, appeared, accompanied by various other aunts, uncles, cousins and other family member and friends. There were tearful kisses and hugs, shaking hands and loud greetings: "Ayo! Ayoka!" Which means 'hello how are you?' I noticed how people took their time saying hello here; the 'ayo, ayokas' between two people could go on for a full five minutes, as they gripped each other by the arms, the greetings becoming ever louder and more expressive: "Ayo, ayooooooooh! Ayooookakakakaka!"

Rocky's mum, Betty, even started dancing, undettered by the rain which had started as we got off the bus and which was getting heavier and heavier. Despite the dark and the rain, I immediately felt very welcome; people were beaming at me, embracing me, or pumping my hand and crying, "Ottowri!" I found out later that this means brother-in-law. Rocky also explained to me that the village of Guédéyo was affectionately called Ottawa, the explanation being, as far as I could understand it, that the village was founded by two separate groups of families, one from Soubré district, the other from Gagnoa. Hence marriages were / are allowed between these two groups, who then become brothers-in-law, which in Bété, the language of this region, is 'Ottowri'. They simply changed this word slightly to 'Ottawa' so that it would have the same name as the Canadian capital. The Canadian ambassador had supposedly visited the village and filmed it.

No one had umbrellas and we were all getting soaked in the rain, so eventually we went inside and they gave us a hearty meal of rice and sauce.

* * *

We were given André's double bed for our stay, in the main room of his house. He slept in an adjoining room on a simple mat on the floor, with one of his three wives. The first night of our stay, despite being very tired after the long day's trip, I didn't sleep that well. The bed, for a start, was very uncomfortable; of the wooden slat type, most of the slats had been broken and replaced by thick branches and whichever way you turned you had a hard branch protruding into your back, the mattress on top being only about three centimetres thick. Then there was the rain which hammered on the corrugated iron roof most of the night. But most of all I had terrible nightmares: there was the dog that had bitten me, which had been amplified into a huge fiery-eyed beast, gripping my arm and when I looked at it, it gradually became engulfed in a black spinning sphere. The sphere appeared perfectly smooth at first but when I looked closer it became more and more coarse, lumpy... until I looked really closely and could see that it was a churning, dirty, mass of organic material. As I looked closer and closer and it became more and more rough, squirming and filthy... I could hear the snarls of animals, human screams... and evil laughter.

I awoke on the first morning of our stay to the sound of laughter, which thankfully sounded innocent enough. It was André and a few of his cronies who were sitting or standing around outside, drinking coffee, chatting, laughing and listening to the radio: very simple music – basic percussion and a man singing, presumably in Bété, their language. I looked at my watch, six a.m. – *ouch, early!* Rocky was stirring too.

"Shall we get up?" I asked her. "It's still early. Six o'clock."

"If you like," she replied, stretching. "Everyone gets up with the sunrise here, if not before."

She looked at my bleary eyes. "You sleep all right?" she enquired.

"Fine," I lied. "Bed's a bit hard, but I suppose we'll get used to it."

We got dressed and before we headed outside, Rocky proposed, "Why don't we give them the gifts now?"

"Okay," I agreed and fished out the two bottles of malt whisky I'd brought. Rocky wheeled out one of the cases of presents.

We said good morning, and I handed over the bottles to her father, who immediately opened them and starting pouring out big tumblers for him and his friends, and one for me, of course. Bit early for the strong stuff, but I chinked glasses and drank with the rest of them. I've never seen whisky disappear so quickly and definitely not at breakfast time.

"Think we'd better get them some beer too," Rocky whispered in my ear. "It's kind of traditional when you arrive somewhere after a long absence."

I consented, and she asked one of her young cousins to bring a couple of crates of beer. Not even seven in the morning and here we were getting tanked on beer and whisky.

Rocky's grandmother, André's mother, Agathe, showed up, grinning like Nelson Mandela. We were introduced and I offered her a glass of whisky, which she gladly accepted. André scowled at this and I heard him muttering something about her getting drunk and saying and doing stupid things. Apparently they were barely on speaking terms, for some reason which I never found out.

The village chief also came over and welcomed us, gladly accepting a nip of whisky and one of the litre bottles of beer that we'd bought. He was a stout, elderly man with a big grey moustache; he reminded me of the village chief from Asterix the Gaul.

Rocky dished out the presents to the relatives that were there that morning; the rest we distributed later that afternoon, either to people that dropped by to André's house or by going directly to their houses.

* * *

For the next ten days I did my best to settle into village life. Amenities in the village were pretty basic. There was no running water in the houses; all the water was obtained from six pumps located at various places in the village. This was used for drinking, washing, cooking, etc. Street lighting was in the process of being installed, but there was no mains electricity in people's homes. A couple of people did have electricity in their houses – generated from petrol-powered turbines. One of them was the village nurse, who had a fridge – to store medicine, a TV and electric lighting in his house. He let kids come and watch the TV in the evening. The other person who had electricity, was Guy, one of André's brothers. He was apparently the most successful of the family, earning a packet off palm-oil plantations. He had electric lights, fans, fridge, TV and even a washing machine. He would install his TV outside in the evening and anytime you passed by you could see ten or so adults sitting in chairs and a few kids crouched down on the ground, all glued to the screen.

There was no telephone anywhere in the village. Supposedly a telephone installation – telephone cabin – was arriving soon. Once there was street lighting and the public telephone, people would then have the possibility to have electricity and telephones in their houses, although only a handful of the more well off people in the village would be able to afford it.

At night, most people used paraffin lamps and torches to see by, notably when eating. People would spend most of their time outside, only really going into their houses to sleep at night. The houses were generally made from a bamboo structure, lashed together with vines, plastered with mud which dried and hardened, and a roof of tarpaulin covered with branches; although some people like André had corrugated metal roofs. There were two or three more well off people who had houses made with bricks or concrete. These included Guy of course. He invited us to stay in his house – it had loads of room, comfortable beds and even a rudimentary shower. I was all for it, but André wouldn't hear of it, his daughter and son-in-law would stay with him and that was final. It was a matter of pride.

André had a half-finished brick extension to his house; for lack of money or will or some other reason, which was never explained to me, the building work had come to a stop. A pile of big grey bricks lay beside the house, gathering weeds. It was here, behind these bricks that I often went for a piss: a nice secluded spot, hidden from the road and other houses by some trees. Pissing here or up against a tree somewhere was fine, but if you needed a crap you had to venture to the 'toilets': basically just a wooden or mud cabin with a hole in the ground – really smelly and nauseating, with flies buzzing around and cockroaches. They were so bad, that one time I propped the unhinged door on its side to let some air in. As I was squatting down, a woman walked past, the chief's wife no less. She saw me, and exclaimed, "Oh my God!" before disgustedly scurrying off. After that incident, I would often just give the toilets a miss and walk into the nearby forest for ten minutes, to have a dump there. For a wash there were other wooden cabins, typically joined on to the toilets. You took in a bucket of warm water, and a smaller bowl for dousing yourself with.

I picked up some basics of the Bété language:

Ayo – Hello

Ayoka – How are you?

Nyom momliba – I'm hungry
Yakili – Let's eat
Nyokom bidou – I'm going for a wash
But most people (apart from the very elderly) spoke decent French, so I communicated largely in French.

* * *

The staple diet was rice, with a little vegetable sauce if you were lucky; rice for breakfast, rice for lunch – although many people skipped lunch, and rice for dinner. People didn't go hungry from what I could see, but there were some people, particularly children, who were evidently suffering from malnutrition: the lack of protein and vitamins. A few had swollen stomachs from eating mainly rice all the time. Meat was a rarity; chicken, the main source of meat, was eaten perhaps once a week, although we were given a lot more. As a sign of respect, people would come and offer me one or two live chickens, which I accepted, taking the chickens by their scaly feet – as was the customary way of saying thanks. Then I handed them over to Betty or Jeanne, who would go off and kill them, pluck them, and cook them. The fresh chicken was delicious, cooked in a spicy sauce with rice or sometimes *aloko* (fried plantain bananas).

Meat being a scarcity, I noticed how every last bit of the chicken, apart from the beak, eyes and crown, was eaten. The intestines were cleaned, fried and then given to the children to eat. The claws and neck were added to the sauce along with the rest. The bones were crunched on and the marrow and juice sucked out of them. Gristle and fat were gladly devoured. In fact, I did feel a bit guilty at being allowed to choose the best bits, like the legs or the wings, and even then someone would sometimes take my left over chicken bones to crunch on.

I was expecting to be given snake or lizard or perhaps insects, but such African stereotypes were not lived up to. We did get to try some more exotic things, like snails, huge ones which had 10 cm diameter shells; frogs – the whole thing, not just the legs; and *viande de brousse* (meat from the forest) – things like squirrels and large rats. Paul, André's other brother, and evidently the poorest of the three, was adept at hunting for such game. He would disappear into the forest on his bike, with his ancient rifle and come back with a dead squirrel strapped to the rack on the back. He also used traps and not just bullets to catch the animals. I didn't sample monkey, thankfully. Supposedly they eat them though, whenever they can find one; but such game is becoming rarer and rarer, since it is over hunted.

Cutlery being a bit of a luxury, people typically ate with their hands, washing them in a basin first. I noticed though that several people would often wash their hands in the same basin of water, dipping them in after the previous guy – hygiene obviously taking a bit of a nose-dive. I usually tried, wherever possible, to wash my hands by pouring on clean water from a basin which no one had used yet or from a bottle of water filled from the pump. We also knew that drinking water from pumps, taps, or elsewhere was inadvisable. So when we didn't have any mineral water, we'd add the anti-bacteria tablets that we'd brought with us to bottles of water from the village pumps, leaving the tablets to dissolve for at least an hour before drinking.

Despite all our precautions, we both had diarrhoea quite a lot, especially me. I had one particularly bad bout halfway through our visit to the village. It lasted three days with fever and vomiting, and was so bad that I had to get medicine and an injection from the village nurse. People were apparently whispering, "Hope we don't lose the white guy." Reassuring.

* * *

Rocky's father, André, was welcoming and civil, although we didn't really converse much. He was kept busy managing his small plantation of palm-oil trees and of course with his three wives: Betty, Jeanne and Carole. Betty, Rocky's mother, was his first wife, then there was Jeanne and finally Carole, whom he'd recently married. Relationships were complicated here. Betty and Jeanne got along fine, but they didn't speak much to the other wife, Carole, the newest one. Carole didn't speak to us either and would just scowl at us whenever our paths crossed; we were considered guilty by association. André also wasn't on speaking terms with his own mother, Agathe, who lived in the house just behind his. I got the impression that he was a rather hard, dour and unforgiving man. He was proud to have me – a white guy, one of the few who had ever come and stayed in the village! – sleep in his house, but was jealous if I went to sit beside and speak to his mother. One afternoon I took her a little bottle of *vin de palmes* – palm wine, made from the fermented sap of palm trees. I then spent a couple of hours chatting to her as we shared the wine. Communication was rather basic, since she didn't speak much French and my Bété was limited to say the least, but I enjoyed her company. She was always radiant, smiling and laughing. When I got back to André's house, Rocky discretely let me know that he was a bit miffed about me giving alcohol to Agathe and that I shouldn't do it again.

Anyway, I tried not to get mixed up in any of the family squabbles. Rocky spent most of her time visiting female cousins, aunts and old friends. After a couple of days I got bored of tagging along for this, and for the rest of the stay I hung out mostly with Jacques and Frédérique, two of André's elder cousins, whom I'd met on our first morning in the village, at the early morning drinking session. I'd immediately taken a shine to them due to their warm, laid back temperament and great sense of humour. They were real salt of the earth, country bumpkin types, with their ripped t-shirts and ancient baseball caps that were all bent, frayed and dusty. We would sit out in front of André's house chatting, listening to the radio and watching the village lizards – margouillats. These things were quite big, up to two feet long, but harmless to people. They were actually a good way of keeping down the insect population. The females were greenish in colour and slightly smaller than the males which were black with orange tails. The males sometimes bobbed their heads up and down, as if they were doing press-ups. I assumed this was some kind of sexual ritual to attract the females.

We also spent a lot of time playing Awalé: a game played with pebbles or grains, and a piece of wood with 10 or 12 holes in it, where the object is to capture as many of the opponents pebbles as possible. The winner is he who captures more than half the total pebbles. Quite easy to learn the basic rules, but difficult to win against more experienced players like Jacques and Frédérique and their cronies. It was also quite amusing to watch them play this; they played at an amazing speed, throwing the pebbles into the holes, the final two pebbles being thrown into two holes at the same time. Jacques in particular was a very exuberant winner. When he won, he would pick up the board and slam it down upside down, as a kind of victorious outburst of joy. Could you imagine chess champions doing this? Checkmate, then wham with the board! Obviously simpler than chess, the game did have some interesting tactics, such as feeding your opponent more pebbles on his side, only to attempt to win them back later; lull him into a false sense of security, only to go in for the kill.

Neither André nor Paul ever played, but the eldest brother, Guy, sometimes did. He was always welcome since he would regularly send out for beer and *coutoucou*, a local strong alcohol made from fermented and distilled sugar cane, and offer it to all the players and spectators present. It was on one such occasion that I first found out about the infamous 'Witch's List.'

"Know how I became so well off?" asked Guy, who had challenged me to a game.

I knew vaguely that it was because he had the biggest

plantation of oil palms but had wondered how he had obtained such a big plantation and how it was so profitable. He certainly didn't seem to do much actual work, but I often saw him directing younger lads here and there to do stuff. I never would have asked him straight up, considering such a question too indiscrete or prying. Plus, I had got used to the Ivoirian custom of always replying to a question with another question: "Why do you ask that?" "In your opinion?" "Who told you this?"

Anyway, he didn't wait for a reply but continued, "I was one of the first to start cultivating oil palms around here. At first we just used the oil ourselves or sold it locally, made a decent living like that. I had the biggest plantation round here and still do. Then big businesses from France and Belgium and Germany started buying the stuff in mass. A few years ago, a German firm set up a production plant down in the next village and I managed to get them to accept all my produce at a reasonable price. Of course I have to renegotiate the price now and again, but I'm a good negotiator so I always get a good deal!"

He grinned, obviously enjoying recounting this tale of his ride to riches. "The best thing though is that all the other plantation owners round here use me to negotiate with the plant and I take a small cut of course. I actually make more money from that than from my own produce."

Ah, one of the famous middlemen.

"How about taking me to see the plantations sometime?" I asked.

"You'd like to see them, would you?" he replied, true to Ivoirian form.

I nodded.

"Well I hardly ever go out to the forests now, but I'm sure Jacques and Frédérique would take you, eh guys?" He nodded to the two of them who were playing Awalé at an adjoining table.

"Sure, Sandy," said Jacques. "We'll take you; let's do it this afternoon."

"Yeah, they still go out there to check on the young workers," continued Guy. "That's how it works round here, the young go out to the fields, the women take care of the housework, and us old guys just live it up!"

Everyone laughed and Guy served up some coutoucou for us all from a big 5-litre jerrycan; it was an actual re-used oil container, it still said Castrol GTX on the side. I downed the stuff, praying that the can had been properly washed out and that I wouldn't be poisoned. Coutoucou wasn't as good as whisky, but I was starting to acquire a taste for the stuff.

"Anyway that's my story, Sandy," Guy went on. "Plus, I always put my trust in God, always say my prayers, always go to church on Sunday. No witchcraft, not like some folk round here."

"What!" I exclaimed. "That stuff really goes on?"

"Of course it does," he said looking ominous. "The dark arts are practised all over the world but especially here in Africa. You know right now there's a girl in this village, down the road there in the hospital, who's very sick, dying. She was on the Witch's List."

"What the heck's that?" I said. "How d'you know it's not just natural causes or something she ate?"

"No. It's because of witchcraft. There's a witch or witches, no one knows who they are for sure, but they have a list, and if your name's on that list it means you're going to die. The witch then gains power for herself or those close to her."

"Hmm, so where's this list?"

"Huh! Who knows? It's all black magic. You know Africa is deep and mysterious. Ah yes, darkest Africa!"

All this talk of witchcraft and black magic had put a bit of a downer on the atmosphere and the players soon finished up their games and headed off for lunch.

* * *

That afternoon, true to their word, Jacques and Frédérique came and fetched me for a walk up to the oil palm plantations. On the main road from Soubré, when you arrive in Guédéyo, the main road forks right through the village, but a small road off to the left leads you up to the school, the hospital, then on towards the forest and the plantations. I'd already walked up this small road before, and a little way into the forest, but this time we walked a lot further into the forest and they took me to the plantations. It all seemed very overgrown to me, but they pointed out the various crops which were being cultivated: cocoa and coffee beans – they let me taste the raw beans, which were surprisingly sweet; sugar cane, which they cut deftly off from the plant using a machete – it was deliciously sweet and crunchy. Finally they took me to an extensive area of huge oil palms. I could see the heavy clumps of orange fruit, from which the oil is extracted, growing below the palms.

They introduced me to some of the young workers. Here, young could mean very young. Children as young as ten were at work with machetes, removing some of the brush which threatened to engulf the food producing plants – the money crops.

"Shouldn't they be in school?" I pointed out. It was a Monday and I was fairly sure the school term had started – I'd heard the noises of children as we passed the school.

"It's the first day of the new term today, actually, but they'd rather be here," said Frédérique. "Wouldn't you, lads?" he shouted to a couple of the youngest looking children.

They just nodded and smiled. Frédérique explained to me that only about fifty per cent of children go to school in the Ivory Coast. They mostly go to school at an early age but many of them drop out due to lack of money to buy books or uniforms, and because their parents want them to work in the fields and also due to the system of *classement*. This is a system whereby pupils have to obtain a mark for the year of at least fifty per cent, to be allowed to move up to the next class. These marks are calculated from exams throughout the year, for various subjects, and also from an end of year exam. An average is computed for each child to decide whether he / she may progress or if he / she will have to repeat the year. This procedure starts from primary school, the age of five upwards, and since typically only half of each year gets the required average mark, this leads to children not advancing quickly enough, and dropping out early or only being educated to a certain level. This *classement* system also leads to the practise of changing birth certificates, he explained. There are cut-off ages at various stages, so for example, to be allowed to attend the equivalent of primary five, you would have to be aged between eight and eleven, and so a twelve-year-old who had doubled a few times would have to change his or her birth certificate so that he or she would 'legally' be ten years old. This method of changing birth certificates is of course illegal, but is such a common practise that even the school teachers actively encourage it, and talk about it openly. I confirmed this during our stay with a young guy, Jean, whom I met in the village. He was 23 years old, but his papers showed him to be 18; he had falsified his papers to be able to complete his secondary school education.

On the way back, they took me to visit the school and the hospital. When we arrived at the school, there was some kind of meeting going on, for the first day back. The parents were standing around the big courtyard in front of the school, where eight classes were lined up in rows of twenty or so to a class, each child putting their hands on the shoulders of the child in front. It was fairly obvious to see the children that had repeated a few times, just by looking at the size differences of children in the same class. We listened to the head teacher giving a speech about how the children had to try harder, parents had to encourage and support their children and take more of an interest in their schooling. Last year's results had been overall pretty poor, with only about half of the pupils in each class advancing, and so on. He also mentioned that the Burkina Faso parents had made a poor job of building a school kitchen, and that if it hadn't been built correctly within the next two weeks – by mid-September, then none of the Burkinabé children would be allowed to attend classes. This blatantly showed the divisions within the village – Burkinabé immigrants, and the few immigrants from places like Mali and Ghana, were treated as second-class citizens. Indeed, I'd noticed how all the immigrants were obliged to live on the south side of the main road, where the land was sloping and the living conditions cramped, while all the locals – the 'pure-blood' Ivoirians – lived on the north side where the land was flat and there was a lot more space, not to mention big, shade providing trees.

These inequalities were visible even amongst the children. The Ivoirian children were mostly wearing school uniforms – white and pink checked dresses for the girls, and khaki shorts and shirts for the boys, or if not they at least wore clean, well fitting dresses, skirts, shorts and t-shirts. While the immigrants' children, mostly Burkinabés, were largely dressed in over-sized t-shirts, ripped and dirty shirts; a few wearing what I suppose you could only describe as rags.

We waited until the end of the little meeting and watched as the children ran and jumped into the arms of smiling parents to be hugged and kissed, before going off home.

As for the hospital, it was just a big dark room with a few beds and drawers containing basic medicines, bandages and needles. The only patient there was the young woman Guy had mentioned. She was writhing and moaning on her bed, as a couple of female carers, from her family I took it, did their best to care for her, mopping her brow with a wet cloth and murmuring soothing words and prayers.

"Poor girl," said Frédérique once we were outside. "The nurse has done all he can. Medicine is no use though, against the witch's power."

"Shouldn't you take her to a real hospital, say in Soubré or Abidjan?" I proposed.

"This *is* a real hospital," said Jacques. "Anyway, according to the nurse, the journey would finish her off. Better that she die here; at least she's in her home village with her family around her. Tragic though, a young woman with her life in front of her. There was talk she was even going to marry the chief."

Marry the chief? Bit young wasn't she? The old codger already had a wife. Oh yeah, I forgot – polygamy was still common here, especially among the elder generations. I kept these thoughts to myself though, and we headed back to the village as the sun was setting.

I heard later that the girl held on for about another week, finally passing away a few days after we'd left the village.

* * *

Sunday arrived and there was church to go to. Mass didn't start until ten, so there was time for a coffee, biscuits and a bowl of cereal; well that's what I ate – the rest of them tucked into bowls of rice.

The churches – there were several of them, as I was about to find out – were all in non-descript little buildings in a lane off the main street, at the other side of the village. We set off at about 9.45 a.m. and had reached the start of the lane, when I realised I'd forgotten my wallet back in André's house. I needed money for the collection, plus I didn't want to leave all our money unattended – the house was unlocked and you never knew, even in a little African village.

"I'm just going to nip back to the house, Rocky," I said. "I forgot the wallet in our room."

She rolled her eyes. "Okay, just hurry up. It's about to start. See you inside."

I quickly went back to the room, picked up the wallet which I'd left inside my little rucksack and made my way back to the lane with the churches. Of course Rocky had forgotten to mention the fact that there were several churches and which one was ours – the Catholic Church. There appeared to be four churches of different denominations; I could hear singing, chanting or muttering of prayers from within four separate buildings – two on the right-hand side of the lane and two on the left. From two of them, the first on the left and the first on the right, I could hear loud vocal 'Hallelujahs' and 'Jesus, my saviour' being cried out, so I presumed these were some sort of evangelical churches. That narrowed it down to two. I could hear prayers or sermons being uttered from within both of them, but the sound was too muffled to make out what was being said. I was just going to have to take potluck. I went into the second church on the right. It was packed inside and I couldn't see any vacant seats. I looked around for Rocky and then I took in the 'priest' or the man leading the proceedings. He was chanting something in a language I couldn't understand – Bété I presumed – and suddenly he picked up a live cockerel by the legs and slashed its throat with a big knife! The congregation then all started loudly chanting something. A few of them were beating their chests. What was this place? Some kind of devil worshipping cult? I didn't wait around to see anymore but discretely left and made for the church on the opposite side of the street – the one second on the right.

Thankfully, this was the right church; Rocky saw me coming in and glared at me. The mass had already started and someone was doing the first reading. I went to sit beside her and whispered, "Sorry, I went into the wrong place. What's going on in that joint across the road? They were sacrificing chickens when I went in."

"Animists," she calmly replied. "I'll explain later."

After mass, she told me that this was some kind of traditional pagan religion. They believe that all humans, animals, plants and even inanimate objects or phenomena have souls or some spiritual essence.

"They sacrifice a lot of chickens, cockerels especially," she explained as if it were perfectly normal. "You just have to accept that things are a bit different here than in Europe. Just relax, enjoy life here in my home village."

Chapter 14

Guédéyo – The Village Idiot: Maybe not so Crazy

The village idiot in Guédéyo was called Kouadjo. As with most village idiots, he was not as stupid as he at first appeared. He would turn up now and again, always with stuff to sell: little trinkets, spices, bananas and other sought after foodstuffs, sometimes even soft or alcoholic drinks. To judge him only by his appearance and demeanour, you would have said, "Yes, this guy is seriously retarded!" It was the way he always stared into space, never looked you in the eye and spoke in a strange mixture of pigeon French and incomprehensible sentences. However, the guy was a seriously good salesman, never aggressive but very persistent, never giving up until you caved in and purchased his wares. He could have sold sand or oil to the Arabs, chopsticks or chop suey to the Chinese, tea or gin and tonics to the English. Once he knew I was Scottish – *how did he know? I didn't tell him anyway* – he got me hooked on these little plastic sachets of whisky. They were not that bad actually – you needed two or three for a decent dram, but they were dirt cheap and tasted good. So he must have earned a decent amount of cash with his wheeling and dealing. All the women of the village not only bought his stuff, but, taking pity on him, gave him free meals: a share of whatever dish was being eaten that day.

The other thing about Kouadjo was that he always seemed to know before anyone else who was on the witch's list. One day, it was just after my bad period of diarrhoea, I was sitting recovering outside in front of the in-laws house, when Kouadjo came along.

"Hi, Kouadjo, how are you?" I greeted him.

"Kouadjo good. Kouadjo got good stuff," he replied and

showed me the little sachets of whisky. There was also some vodka and gin.

"Okay. Give me six of the whisky, six vodka and skip the gin – what d'you take me for? An Englishman?"

"Here. Bananas. Try some."

I unpeeled one of the small sweet bananas he'd offered and ate it. It was delicious. They'd probably help prevent diarrhoea too. "Okay, I'll buy a bunch."

"You buy three bunches. Nice! Cheap. Only one hundred francs CFA a bunch."

"Okay, I'll take two bunches if you like."

"Three. Share with wife."

"Okay, Kouadjo, you convinced me." I paid him for the bananas.

"Gladys on list," he muttered.

"What?"

"Gladys, Jonah wife, she on witch list. Here come the commandos!"

He was always going on about the 'commandos.' I ignored that part and asked him to explain about the list. "What do you mean, she's on the list? Who's Gladys? How do you know this, Kouadjo?"

"Bye," was all he replied, and then he got up and left.

* * *

A bit later, I asked my wife, as she was munching her way through her fifth banana, if she knew anyone in the village by the name of Gladys.

"Yes, Gladys, the village chief, Jonah's wife," she replied.

"Kouadjo just told me she's on the witch's list. Does this list really exist? Surely Kouadjo's not involved?"

"Oh, it exists all right. People say you can pay with money, a blood offering or by doing some favour for the witch and then you can chose a person to put on the list or get her to perform some other black magic deeds. As for Kouadjo, don't ask me – probably has some sixth sense or something."

"Black magic, blood offerings! Do you actually believe this bullshit? Who is this witch, where does she live? Does she fly around on a broom?"

"Don't be daft, Sandy! They say she's hidden deep in the forest. Might not even be a woman, could be a man or a beast or some kind of supernatural spirit."

"Has this got anything to do with those chicken sacrificing freaks I saw last Sunday?"

"What the animists? No. Their magic is nowhere near as powerful as the witch's."

"This is just nuts!" I exclaimed.

"No. This is Africa."

"So what's going to happen to Gladys then?"

"If she's on the list, she'll probably get sick and die. That's what happens to people on the list. Or they meet with a nasty accident, or just drop dead."

"Couldn't it just be natural causes? Enhanced maybe by some kind of psychological terror, if the person thinks they're on the list and are going to die?"

"Whatever, Sandy. Believe what you want. But it exists, I'm telling you."

* * *

Later that afternoon, I was just sitting around in the courtyard in front of André's house, when Jacques and Frédérique came along and asked me to come with them for a drink somewhere else. So off we went down the road a bit, to one of the places that sold beer. I suppose you could call these places maquis, but they were nothing like the big professional establishments in Abidjan. They were just someone's house with a few crates of beer inside and a table and chairs outside, in the shade of trees or an overhanging roof which acted as a parasol.

The guy who owned this particular place was from Burkina Faso and had tribal scars decorating his face, as did many of the immigrants from Burkina Faso or Mali. He set down a big litre bottle of *Flag Spéciale* – locally made beer, and three glasses which were covered in dust.

"Hey! The glasses! Go and rinse them!" Frédérique ordered.

He came back and plonked the cleaned glasses on the table then strode off without a word.

"These Burkinabés," said Jacques.

"Yeah, what are they like," agreed Frédérique and they both shook their heads.

Jacques, with typical exuberance, used a bottle opener on the beers in a strange way, so that the top flew off making a sound like the cork popping off a bottle of champagne. He poured out the beer like some Arab pouring tea, lifting the bottle high above the glass, so as to get the beer all frothy on top. "*Il faut que ça mousse!*" he cried. Rough translation – "You need a good head on your beer!"

They got back on to the subject of immigrants. "These Burkinabés should know their place," said Frédérique. "One of them even wants to become president of our country, can you imagine?"

"Yeah, the sheer balls," said Jacques. "Ouattara. He was born here, but his parents are Burkinabés. His dad anyway. Makes him a Burkinabé in my book."

"Yeah, they can come here to do manual work if they like," continued Frédérique. "But that's it. No government jobs. No businesses. No marrying our women."

What about me? I thought. *I'm a foreigner married to one of your women.* Apparently that was okay, though, because I was white, a European. A strange form of racism was at work here. Although I doubted they'd let me become president either; nor one of our children, not that it looked likely that Rocky and I would ever have children.

"Have you noticed, Sandy, how the best land in the village is kept for us Ivoirians, us pure Bétés?" said Frédérique.

"Yes," I replied meekly. I didn't want to get into an argument about racism with my two new friends.

"The immigrants all stay on the other side of the road and that's the way it is," said Jacques.

"I noticed that Abdelah has opened a little shop just in front of André's house," I said, working up the courage to contradict them slightly. "He's Burkinabé, isn't he?"

It was actually more of a kiosk than a shop, selling drinks, sweets and snacks. He'd opened it a couple of days after our arrival and had come round offering everyone free sweets, to drum up interest in his little business. For the moment it was just open in the evenings; he was off working on the plantations like most of the other young immigrants during the day.

"I doubt that'll last long," said Frédérique. "And he had to pay baksheesh to André." Ah, the famous African baksheesh or bribe.

We shared five big bottles of beer between the three of us, and a couple of shots of coutoucou each. Afternoon turned into evening and with the setting sun, the field workers started arriving home from a tiring day's work on the plantations. Suddenly we heard a big commotion a few houses down the street: men shouting and women wailing. We finished our drinks and walked down towards the source of the noise, to see what was going on. The bloodied body of Abdelah was laid out before his house, which he shared with his sister and the sister's husband and their two young children. He'd apparently been hacked to death by machetes out by the plantations. Some of his Burkinabé workmates had found his dead body and brought it back to the village.

As we approached, the Burkinabés assembled around his body started shouting at us in Dyula. I couldn't understand anything, but it was clear we weren't welcome, so we made our way back to André's house.

There were a lot of young male villagers gathered out in his courtyard; André was nowhere to be seen. Jean, one of Rocky's old classmate friends, who worked out in the plantations, filled us in on what had happened. Abdelah had apparently made some advances towards one of the Ivoirian women: a certain Isabelle – a strikingly beautiful young girl whom I'd met a couple of times in the village. He'd even gone so far as to ask her to marry him. The problem was that another young man, Pierre – a Bété, had his eye on the girl too, and had also been about to propose. Jealousy had turned ugly and Pierre had assembled a posse of a few of his friends and they'd set upon the poor Abdelah with machetes; he'd had no chance. The divisions, the tensions and the jealousy in the village had boiled over into murderous violence.

Rocky turned up and I took her aside.

"What's going to happen to the killers?" I asked her. "Have the police been informed?"

"That's not how it works round here," she declared matter-of-factly. "The nearest police are in Soubré. This will probably be handled by the chief and his committee of village elders."

All of whom were locals I gathered.

"Committee, village elders?" I asked incredulously. "Those guys need to go in prison. It was cold-blooded murder!"

"The killers will be punished, and they will probably have to pay blood money to Abdelah's family. But Pierre is the chief's nephew. There's no way he's going to let him go to prison."

"This is just madness! We have to leave," I said firmly. "We're leaving tomorrow."

"No, Sandy, we're not," replied Rocky, coldly. "I need a few more days with my family. We can leave at the weekend, Saturday if you like."

It was Wednesday. Would we survive that long?

"We may be in danger, don't you realise, Rocky. D'you know André took a bakchich from Abdelah to let him set up his little stall. Who knows if those thugs won't take their fury out on us next!"

"We're in no danger, don't worry," she tried to reassure me.

"And all this stuff about witchcraft and witch's lists, what if it's just people poisoning each other?" I ranted on. "Maybe I was even poisoned. I was sick for three days in case you didn't notice. No witchcraft required."

"Don't be daft, you just had bad diarrhoea," she reasoned. "You're being paranoid. I went to school with Jean and Pierre and all that lot, they're mostly all right."

"Mostly all right! They just hacked a guy to death."

"We don't know what really happened. Maybe Abdelah attacked Pierre and he just defended himself."

"Yeah, right."

I saw there was no point in reasoning with her. I thought about leaving without her on the first baca out of there the next morning. It would probably spell the end of our marriage, but maybe that was for the best. My notion that this trip might somehow re-kindle our marriage was proving completely flawed. Still no sex – how long had it been? Five, six months? She was colder than ever towards me.

Despite everything, I decided to stay. It was years since she'd seen her family after all. Maybe our marriage could still be saved. There were still two and a half weeks left before our return flight, and Rocky had talked about doing some touristy stuff – the beautiful beaches of San Pedro, the Basilica of Yamoussoukro. If we could spend a few days, just the two of us, in a more laid back and relaxing setting, then perhaps it could work wonders on our relationship.

Chapter 15

Guédéyo – Cockroaches and Killers

After a restless night, I was woken by the crowing of cockerels and the sounds of people getting up, preparing fires, cooking rice and so on. I was needing a crap and was about to take a quick walk into the forest, but Jeanne saw me heading off and waved at me to come over. There was no sign of André and Rocky was still sleeping.

"Just use the toilets, Sandy," she said. "Don't worry; I've just put some detergent in. It's a lot less smelly."

"Ah, okay. Thanks." I smiled at her.

"Here. Here's your water for the bathroom after." She handed me a big bucket of water that had been heated up on the fire, with the little scoop bucket inside which you used for dousing yourself.

"Thanks a lot, Jeanne."

The disinfectant she'd sprayed had worked wonders, the toilet actually smelled fresh and perfumed. I was doing my business when I vaguely sensed things moving in the hole down below – one of them crawled out – they were huge three inch long cockroaches! I hastily finished up, but by this time there were two or three cockroaches crawling around. Disgusting! The things must feed on the faeces and the detergent had irritated them. I closed the toilet door behind me as firmly as possible and headed to the little adjoining wash-cabin.

I undressed, doused myself with water, shampooed my hair and was just lathering myself with soap, when I noticed about six big cockroaches crawling through a gap at the top of the wall, which separated the toilet from the washroom. I attempted to kill them by hitting them with a bit of wood – this was quite difficult, since the things appeared virtually indestructible. I ended up having to grind them to a pulp or decapitate them before they stopped crawling around. I continued soaping myself, but I looked up again and saw dozens of the cockroaches crawling through the gap! Needless to say I tried to kill as many of these as I could, but it turned out that these things could actually fly too! They also had large pincers and some landed on me and started pinching me on different parts of my body but mostly around my forehead and eyes, probably because that was the only part of me which wasn't covered in soap. I desperately tried to keep them out of my eyes. As I brushed them away off my eyebrows, I could see blood on my hands. Their pincers were like little knifes! I had to get out of there. I stumbled naked and half-blind out of the bathroom and as I did so, several lizards, which had been crawling up the walls, the roof and the doorway jumped on top of me to try and eat the cockroaches. "Aaaaaaarrrrgh!" I screamed.

My scream was matched by that of a woman. Most of the cockroaches were now gone, flown off, eaten by the lizards or killed by me, so I could see more clearly. It was Gladys, the chief's wife, again.

"Oh my God! Oh my God!" she cried as she hurried off up the lane towards her house.

A couple of the lizards had even gone into the bathroom and were feasting on the rest of the cockroaches. I just grabbed the bucket of water, dowsed myself in one go, then put a towel round my waist and went back, dripping and bleeding to André's house. Rocky was there, but didn't seem overly concerned by my state. It was Jeanne who screamed when she saw me. It was she who helped me to a seat.

"What happened?" she asked with concern.

"Cockroaches and lizards," I explained. "In the bathroom. Don't bother with the detergent next time."

Rocky went off and got our first-aid kit. I could feel my eyes swelling up. She disinfected the places on my body where the cockroaches had pinched me, then applied a couple of bandages to my eyebrows – where the worst of the damage was.

"Just a few scratches, you'll be fine," she said.

I just glared at her. I wanted out of this place!

She read my mind. "Don't worry, Sandy. We're leaving on Saturday, the day after tomorrow. We can head to Yamoussoukro."

* * *

For the remainder of the day, I just rested out in the courtyard. My head was throbbing and my eyes so swollen I could hardly see. Jacques and Frédérique dropped by to say hello but were a lot more subdued than usual. The atmosphere in the whole village was very morose after yesterday's killing.

"The trial is this afternoon," Jacques informed me.

"Shouldn't you just take the killers to the police in Soubré?" I asked.

"That's not how we do things round here," he replied.

"Except in extreme circumstances," said Frédérique.

How much more extreme did you need? I wondered if it was the other way round – a Burkinabé killing a local Bété – what would happen. A different story, no doubt. He would without question be sent off to the police, if he wasn't lynched here first.

"Don't worry, they'll get a fair trial," said Jacques, ever proud of the village facilities and way of doing things. "Just as good as what they'd get in Soubré, before an official judge. Our village elders won't be lenient."

"Yeah, you never know, tonight we may be in for a hanging," said Frédérique jokingly and motioned an imaginary rope round his neck being pulled up, while he closed his eyes and stuck out his tongue.

This time, for once, no one laughed at his antics.

* * *

Everyone who wasn't busy working in the forest made their way to the trial at four p.m. I thought about going, but I was still feeling terrible, so when Rocky proposed that I come along I declined.

"I'll give it a miss. I'll just hang out here and rest."

"Okay. We're all going, except Jeanne. She'll get you something to eat later. These things can go on a long time."

So I was left in the company of Jeanne and her little two-year-old boy, Benoît. She was actually the nicest of André's three wives, always smiling, teaching me Bété and teasing me, so I enjoyed spending that late afternoon and evening with her, while the rest of the village was off for the trial. We chatted while she gave little Benoît a wash, soaped him down and rinsed him off right there in the courtyard. If only I could just wash here instead of in the wash-cabin, where I'd been attacked by cockroaches, but I suppose modesty prevented that.

"Sorry about your little mishap this morning," she said. "I can change your bandages if you want."

"That's okay, Jeanne," I replied. "Wasn't your fault, although I wouldn't bother with disinfectant the next time. Think the bandages should be fine until tomorrow." I wasn't really looking forward to getting them off, because I knew it would probably rip out half my eyebrows.

"Did you just decide to put the disinfectant in yourself or did someone tell you?" I asked.

"Someone," she admitted.

"Who?"

But she just looked away. I knew there was no way I'd coax the name of the culprit out of her, but I suspected Carole, the third wife. She was always glowering at me; I wouldn't be surprised if she was the witch or one of the witches or poisoners.

"Come and see what I've got you for dinner," she said, changing the subject.

She led me in to her little hut; each of the wives had a little hut with a wood fire and a mat where they slept when they weren't with André. The place was so thick with smoke my eyes immediately starting watering and what with that and the swelling from the cockroach incident they closed up completely. She led me towards the stove and placed my hand on something. I felt feathers and heard the thing clucking. It was a live chicken, tethered up by one of its feet to the stove. The ultimate humiliation, tied up to the steaming pot in which you are about to be cooked.

"I got a really nice chicken, just for you," she said.

"Thanks, Jeanne," I coughed. I couldn't wait to get out of that hut. God knows how she could stand cooking in that place.

Around six p.m. she made me hold the chicken by its feet while she slit its throat, then when it had stopped writhing around, she plucked it and went off to cook it.

Little Benoît got some fried intestines as an appetiser and around seven, the three of us had a hearty dinner of rice and chicken cooked in a spicy red sauce. The sun had set but there was still no sign of anyone coming back from the trial. It was very quiet, just the sound of Benoît gagooing away and the ever-present hum of the cicadas.

When Jeanne took Benoît off to bed, I decided to take a walk. The trial was being held in the village committee building, which was further up in the lane, where the churches were; it was just a big open space covered by a thatched roof, held up by big wooden posts; walls didn't seem necessary. As I walked past the lane, I could hear raised voices. I kept on going along the main road. After a while I noticed some smoke coming from a little clearing surrounded by trees. As I went closer I could hear someone muttering. I went over to see who it was – Kouadjo, sitting by himself and looking into an open wood-fire.

"The commandos, the commandos, the commandos…" he repeated over and over again.

He stopped his ranting when he heard me coming and

looked up.

"How are you, Kouadjo?" I enquired

"Fine. You buy whisky?" he replied, ever the salesman.

"Okay, give me a couple of sachets," I consented. We drank one each there by the fire.

"You been up at the trial? Heard anything about what's going on?" I said, just to be conversational, not expecting to get any sense out of him.

"Off to the commandos," he said.

"What is it with you and the commandos?"

He didn't reply. We just sat there staring into the fire for a while. Then suddenly there were the sounds of people arriving: footsteps, voices. About ten young men arrived and sat down beside us by the fire – it was Pierre, his fellow accused and a few of his supporters. They were visibly upset, some of them cursed in French or Bété, others spat into the fire, others just sat there shaking their heads and looking shocked.

Once they'd settled down a bit, I cleared my throat and dared to ask the question: "So what happened at the trial?"

"One million francs CFA to pay as blood money! Each!" said Pierre. "And since none of us have anything like that money, they're forcing us to sign up to the army for five years and send back half our wages."

The army – the commandos! Looked like Kouadjo wasn't so mad on this occasion.

"Practically a death sentence," said Lacroix, one of Pierre's main henchmen.

"It's all André's fault," said Pierre. "He was the one that pushed for this severe sentence. He's on the Burkinabé's side I'm sure. The chief was proposing a more lenient punishment – a tenth of that blood money, to be paid over ten years and two years community work around the village."

"Didn't the chief get the final word?" I asked.

"Halfway through the trial, when the debate was in full flow, the chief started coughing and spluttering," explained Pierre. "He was so bad he had to be taken to his bed. Before leaving he delegated his power to André."

"Yeah and look at what he's dished out to us," said Lacroix. "Fate worse than death. At least hanging would be quicker. Anyone that's ever joined the army from this village has ended up dead."

"And it'll be worse now, since the *coup d'état*," said Pierre.

He was referring to the military takeover which happened in December 1999.

"Haven't things settled down now?" I asked. "That was almost three years ago and you now have a new president, Gbagbo isn't it?"

"No, things haven't *settled down*," said Pierre. "That *coup d'état* was just the beginning. Gbagbo won, but most of the opposition candidates weren't allowed to stand. Outtara still has his eyes on the presidency. Son of a Burkinabé!" He spat out the word 'Burkinabé' to show his disgust.

"Power grabbing scum," he continued. "Just like André here. He wants to out the chief and take his place. It's obvious. I reckon he's the witch. First the chief's new fiancé falls ill and now the chief himself."

The others grunted in agreement.

"Plus he supports the Burkinabés," added Lacroix. "Look at the sentence we've been handed out, just for protecting our own!"

"André's the witch!" I tell you shouted Pierre. "It must be him or he must at least be in cahoots with the witch!"

Lacroix leapt up and grabbed a big stick; how easily firewood became a makeshift weapon. "Let's get him! Teach the bastard a lesson!" he shouted. He was the biggest and strongest of all the young men present; his biceps rippled in anger.

"Calm down guys. André hasn't done anything wrong. He's completely innocent!" I tried to reason with them.

But my pleadings had no effect. Pierre also grabbed a stick and shouted, "Lacroix's right, we can't let him get away with this! Let's get him! Who's with me?"

Pierre, Lacroix, the two other convicted and most of the others who'd been sitting at the fire all made off – armed with sticks, batons or machetes – towards André's house. I followed behind them with the rest of the fire sitters who didn't want to be part of the lynch mob. Did we intend to intervene or just witness what was about to be meted out to André? I never got to find out. When we arrived at André's house, he'd already left, somehow getting wind of the posse which was after him. After having searched the house and the huts of his three wives, who shouted insults at them in Bété, they stood around in the courtyard for a few minutes, looking disgruntled.

Pierre interrogated the wives, but none would say more than that he'd left about fifteen minutes ago.

"He's no doubt gone to hide in the forest," Pierre remarked.

"Let's go after him," suggested Lacroix.

"Forget it, we'll never find him in this dark," said Pierre. "Plus, he knows the forest intimately, better than any of us. We'll get him when he shows up."

They all headed back to the fire. I tagged along, for want of anything better to do. Rocky was nowhere to be seen; had she fled with her father, to help him hide and take care of him?

Back at the fire they all sat dejectedly, muttering curses in French and Bété. After a few minutes, there was a rustling noise behind the firewood. It was a huge rat. Pierre and a few of his gang leapt up and killed the rat by hitting it with wooden sticks. Was this what would have happened to André if he hadn't disappeared? Lacroix got out a big knife and proceeded to skin the dead rodent; they were planning to roast it on the fire and eat it. I decided to leave.

* * *

Pierre and his fellow convicts didn't obtain another chance to get André. An army patrol turned up early next morning, accompanied by André. God knows how he'd got hold of them so quickly. Abdelah's murderers were rounded up and led off at gunpoint to join the army. They all hung their heads as they left, as if they were being led to the gallows; all but Pierre who defiantly shouted, "Witch!" at André as he was led towards the army truck. He received a boot up the backside for his outburst from one of the army sergeants, and then he was bundled into the truck with the rest. I actually noticed André smiling for the first time since we arrived, as the army convoy sped off in a cloud of dust.

Rocky had shown up in our bedroom in André's house sometime after midnight. She hadn't offered an explanation and I hadn't bothered to ask. The rest of the day passed without event. We packed our bags and said goodbye to family and friends in the village. In the afternoon I went for a final drink with Frédérique and Jacques. The Burkinabé side of the village was best avoided after the recent events, so we found a local improvised maquis further up the road, on the Bété side, who supplied us with a table, chairs and beer.

"We're going to miss you, Sandy," said Frédérique. "Where are you headed next?"

"San Pedro or Yamoussoukro, I think," I replied. "I've liked it here in the village; I'm going to miss you guys too."

This wasn't really a lie, despite all that had happened. I did actually like the life in the village, mishaps and angry mobs excepted. Drinking and playing awalé with the old guys, going for walks in the forest, the openness and generosity of the people – all this I would miss enormously. You could basically go and say 'hi' to anyone in the village, and they would welcome you into their courtyard and give you a seat to sit down on and offer you some food. One day I'd just been strolling through the village, and an old guy had greeted me from his courtyard; he was blind in one eye, dressed in rags and walked laboriously with the help of a cane. He immediately broke the piece of corn on the cob he was eating and gave me half.

"To Guédéyo, Ottawa!" I proposed a toast and we chinked glasses.

"You should come back here when things have calmed down a bit," suggested Frédérique. "You'll always be welcome. Even come and live here if you like."

"Yeah," agreed Jacques. "Abidjan, Paris, London, even New York – all just *poudre aux yeux*!" Literally, powder in the eyes; rough translation – window dressing. "You'd be better off settling down here, get yourself a couple more wives, live the good life!"

How would I support them, never mind myself?

Frédérique read my thoughts. "With a little money you can plant oil palms. Then just pay a few young folk to manage and harvest them. Think about it. You could be relaxing here in the village, instead of rushing around in the pollution of Paris."

I said I'd think about it. However outlandish and far-fetched it sounded, a small part of me actually wanted to do what they suggested.

The sun set, we parted company and I went back to André's for dinner before turning in for an early night. We planned to catch an early morning baca to Soubré before heading to Yamoussoukro for a few days, then San Pedro, then back to Abidjan. At least that was the plan.

Chapter 16

Guédéyo – A Moonlit Walk

I awoke during the night with the strange sensation that something was different. I lay there in the darkness of our room for a few minutes before I realised what it was – total silence. The usual music of the cicadas and all the other night-time cacophony – insects, lizards, rodents, night-birds – was absent, leaving a strange silence in the village. I got up and had a look outside; no one was around. I took a leak at my usual place beside the big pile of bricks and gazed up at the night sky, there was a beautiful moon and a stunning spectacle of stars. Wide-awake by then, I decided to go for a walk. I headed off down the path towards the forest, the only noise was that of my own footsteps and breathing. Bizarre.

When I had almost reached the forest, I suddenly heard the unmistakable sound of an owl hooting. "Twitawoo, who are you, how do you do?" she seemed to be saying, as if beckoning me towards her.

I headed along the path into the forest, towards the call of the owl. It was darker in the forest and I cursed myself for not bringing a torch, but thanks to the light of the full moon, I could make my way without too many problems. Just when it felt as if I was almost upon the owl, the source of the call seemed to move on, leading me at first along the main path, then onto narrower, more overgrown paths. I didn't feel overly frightened, even if at the back of my mind were thoughts about what or who I could come across in this forest, as I made my way deeper and deeper – wild animals, poisonous vegetation… even the witch, if he or she existed; the call of the owl was somehow both enticing and reassuring.

Eventually, just as the path was getting almost impassable

and I'd started hacking at the undergrowth with a big stick to be able to continue on my way, the call stopped. I continued on a few meters and arrived at a huge clearing in the forest. Suddenly I heard the flap of wings and saw the owl, pure and white in the moonlight, flying off above the trees in the direction I'd just come. It was then that I noticed a chink of light in the middle of the clearing. As I walked towards it I saw that it was an open fire and there seemed to be someone sitting beside it!

I approached cautiously. Was this the infamous witch? Had she put some kind of spell on me to attract me into the forest, where she would perform some fiendish rites upon me or sacrifice me to some evil spirits? When I drew nearer I could see that it was an old woman; she looked up and smiled at me.

"Welcome, Sandy. Sit down and warm yourself by the fire."

"Hello. How do you know my name? Who are you?" I suddenly felt the cold; I was dressed only in thin pyjamas and flip-flop sandals. I could feel myself shivering from a mixture of cold and fear. My desire for warmth overcame my fear and I sat down hesitantly by the fire.

"My name is Sandra. I'm a *féticheur*."

"What's that? Some kind of witch?"

"I have the same powers as a witch, but I use them for good, not for bad; to help others, not for my own personal gain. I'm a traditional healer if you like."

"And you live out here, in the forest?"

"Yes. The forest provides – fruit and vegetables, the odd bird or squirrel or monkey. And some of the people who come to me bring me food too."

"Did you summon me? The owl – was that you?" It seemed crazy, but what other explanation was there.

She may have been a witch or a healer, but true to Ivoirian form, she answered my question with another question. "Do you believe in witches, in supernatural powers?" She looked at me intensely; her eyes appeared to be the same colour as the fire; or was it just the reflection?

Despite everything that had happened on the trip and before, I still didn't really believe. Although sitting there by the fire, looking into the mysterious eyes of this ancient woman, her face a thousand wrinkles, the immensity of the African night around us, the silence broken only by the crackling of burning wood, my remaining scepticism started to evaporate.

"Yes. I do. I'm starting to."

"It's real, Sandy. Evil witchcraft exists and is at work here."

"Who's the witch? André? His new wife, Carole?"

"Unfortunately for you, I can't tell you now – it's too dangerous. But you'll eventually find out, much later, who the witch is. Then you'll be able to exact your revenge."

"Revenge for what? What do you mean?"

"Look for the sign, the sign written in blood made to the devil. And the sacrifice." She shuddered, then starting shaking a necklace of what looked like animal bones and chanting something in a language I couldn't understand. It didn't seem to be Bété.

What sign? What sacrifice? What was she talking about? I wanted to ask her more questions, but her chanting was strangely hypnotic and I found myself looking entranced into the flames, which danced seemingly in time to her incantations.

After a while – ten minutes, an hour? I don't know how long I stared into that fire – I was aware that the chanting had stopped. I shook my head and came out of my trance-like state. The woman was gone. Sandra. Almost like Sandy.

The fire had died down to a bed of glowing embers and I began to feel cold again, so I got up and headed back to Guédéyo; to André's house. I had no owl to guide me, but somehow I found my way back with no problems. The village was still asleep, silent. Only once I'd closed the door and got into bed, did I hear the cicadas begin to sing again.

Chapter 17

N'Koupé

The next morning we made our tearful farewells to Rocky's family. Well, all of her family that is, except her mum, Betty who joined us as we got on the baca at eight a.m.

"She's coming with us?" I asked Rocky. "To Yamoussoukro?"

"We're not going to Yamoussoukro," she replied. "At least not yet anyway. We just found out that Mum's cousin, Adèle, has died. We're going to attend the funeral ceremonies, back in her home village, N'Koupé."

"N'Koupé? Where the heck's that?"

"It's over more towards the east side of the country, near the town of Adzopé. Don't worry it's not that far."

Not that far? We arrived eight hours later: a two hour bone-busting ride along the dirt roads in the first baca to Soubre, another bigger bus to Gagnoa, then another change. The longest stretch was from Gagnoa to Adzopé, stopping at what seemed like a hundred towns and villages along the road. Then finally we had to get another little baca for an hour, to get out to the village of N'Koupé, in the suburbs of Adzopé.

Funerals in Ivory Coast were an altogether different affair from the sober, dignified, black-suited ceremonies which I was used to back in Scotland, where any displays of emotion were generally suppressed, even tears choked back. When we arrived in the village, events were already in full swing. A crowd of women were parading up and down the main thoroughfare, swaying in time to the beat of a couple of djembés, their faces painted white with what looked like clay. They wailed, sang and chanted; and every so often one of the deceased's relatives or friends would break down in tears, ripping their clothes or even rolling around on the dusty ground. This was what they referred to as the 'dance of death.'

Rocky and her family ran off to join them, leaving me to my own devices. I got talking to a group of youths who were hanging around in the shade of some palm trees, including Sonia, one of the defunct's step-daughters. She was startlingly beautiful, her skin a smooth, unblemished, dark brown, her hair cropped short, dressed in a simple, loose, yellow dress, no makeup, jewellery or other artifices.

"Here have some of this." She offered me a slice of mango.

"Thanks!" The fruit was succulent and delicious. "We don't get mangos like those in Scotland."

"Hmm, yes, Scotland, very far off. Try one of these aubergines." She smiled coyly, handing me a small, round vegetable which I recognised as a chilli pepper, one of the extremely hot Caribbean varieties.

"I may be from Scotland, but I'm not daft. That's a chilli pepper. What are you trying to do, kill me?"

She just laughed. "Aubergine! Go on, try it, it's nice!"

"I'd rather have some more mango."

So she strolled to a nearby mango tree, and using a simple tool of a knife attached to a long stick, deftly cut me off a lovely, fresh, ripe mango.

"Here, just for you." She cut the mango into slices using a machete and gave them to me.

"Yum, that *is* good!"

"Why don't we take a ride into the forest and I can show you even better fruit trees: mango, pineapple, banana."

"Okay." I didn't need much persuasion.

She borrowed a motorbike from one of the other youths and we rode off. She drove and as I gripped onto her firm waist, taking in her sweet perfume, I felt more and more aroused. She took me deep into the jungle, ditching the bike at one point and leading me along a dirt path, having to hack away now and again at the vegetation, to make headway. We eventually arrived at a small clearing, where there were all the kinds of fruit trees she'd mentioned and more – some so exotic I couldn't even recognise them. But by this point I was only interested in the exotic fruits of her body.

We began fondling and kissing each other, and then playfully took off each other's clothes. Her body against mine felt so smooth and pure. We made love right there in the jungle, our moans blending in with that of the other wildlife – the buzzing insects, the squawking birds and the screeches of monkeys.

On her second orgasm, I felt her nails digging deeply into my thighs; so much so that she drew blood on the right thigh. I looked at her face and all I could see were the whites of her eyes, as if she were possessed.

"Sorry!" she said as she saw my bleeding leg, and began mopping up the blood with a Lotus paper handkerchief.

"I'm not," I replied. "I want to marry you and take you back to France."

"I think your wife, Rocky, might have a few objections."

"Less than you think. Our marriage is on its last legs."

She just looked away bashfully.

* * *

It was getting dark as we made our way back to the village. Sonia gave the motorbike back to the guy from whom she'd borrowed it, then she stayed on chatting to some of her friends, while I went back to the house we were staying in; her dad's house. It was a big construction, made of bricks, with a wooden porch at the front.

Rocky, Betty, Lambert (Adèle's husband, Sonia's dad) and a few other family members were sitting on the porch chatting. I joined them. The actual burial would be tomorrow morning, so we were planning to stay at least two more nights. When I went to get a sweatshirt out of the bedroom where we'd be sleeping,

Rocky followed me in.

"Been enjoying yourself then?" she said, looking at me knowingly.

How could she know about Sonia and me? We'd been very discrete. I suppose someone may have told her that we'd left together on the motorbike, in the direction of the jungle.

"Just chatting to some of the young guys," I replied. "Took a motorbike ride to get some fruit in the jungle."

"Hope you liked the *ride* and the *fruit*," she said looking at me mockingly.

She knew or at least suspected that I'd been unfaithful. She didn't seem overly concerned. Was our marriage really over in her eyes? I was beginning to see that rekindling our love wasn't part of her plans for this trip.

* * *

The next day there was a big funeral procession through the village, similar to the previous day's 'dance of death,' but slightly more subdued and dignified. All the women, including Rocky, painted their faces and arms with white mud or clay, and danced in a kind of slow shuffling movement through the main road of the village. Sonia, aged eighteen, was considered too young for this ritual, but we stood close to each other on the roadside and watched, casting furtive glances at each other now and again. Then there was a big funeral mass, which lasted about two hours, with all the singing, the prayers and the eulogising. Finally, the coffin containing Adèle's remains was carried about a kilometre, to a decrepit little cemetery, full of ancient crumbling gravestones and simple wooden crosses. Here there were the final prayers and the burial. No flowers. Even if there were some available, it would have been pointless in the intense heat. Some of her family just laid palm leaves on top of the grave.

Then it was back to Lambert's house for lunch and chatting.

Mostly in French, but also sometimes in Bété or Attié – the region's local language, which sounded nothing like Bété. Sometimes they also spoke in a French dialect called Nouchi, which I could barely understand, although sometimes I could guess the meaning of what was being said by the hand gestures.

I was introduced to Sonia's mother, Clara, Lambert's second wife, after the now deceased Adèle. He also had two more: Tatiana and Gloria. Clara showed me how to remove the husks of rice – 'pilling' as they called it. You take a piece of wood, shaped kind of like a big baseball bat, and pound the rice in a large standing wooden bowl, until all the yellow husky stuff has been removed and it appears white. I had a go – it was quite hard work, especially in the thirty-five degree heat. Once all the husks are off, they put the mixture in a huge flat tray or plate and separate the husks from the rice by hand. It seemed like a huge amount of effort just to get a few bowls of rice. Reading my mind, Clara informed me that some villages now had machines to do all the pilling and separating, but they were very expensive so were few and far between.

Like in Guédéyo, there was no electricity, or running water. It was more or less the same deal. Water was obtained from a well, using a foot-pump. Only one or two people had electric generators. The dwellings were mainly traditional dried-mud houses, but there were a few more brick or concrete buildings – like Rocky's Uncle Lambert's house, where we slept.

* * *

That night before going to sleep, Rocky informed me that we were going to San Pedro next. Her mum would stay on here for a bit longer.

"Okay, what about Yamoussoukro?" I asked.

"We can go there after," she said. "San Pedro's really nice. Beautiful beaches. Delicious fish and seafood. You'll like it."

It seemed a bit crazy, distance and time-wise. We'd be swinging all the way down to the south-west for San-Pedro, then back up to the centre for Yamoussoukro, but I couldn't be bothered challenging her. Beaches, relaxing, grilled fish and seafood – it did sound good.

Rocky was soon in the land of slumber, but I couldn't get to sleep. My head was buzzing with the sounds of all the strange languages I'd heard today and the haunting chants of the funeral ceremonies. I decided to get up and have a walk. It was a clear night, but very dark – the moon was mostly concealed by clouds. Having no electric streetlights, you really did need a torch or lamp to see your way around at night, but I waited for my eyes to adjust, then walked slowly. After a while the clouds dispersed and in the night sky I could see a glorious bright moon and thousands of stars, the most beautiful starlit sky I've ever seen.

I found myself walking along the road which led to the cemetery. I didn't plan to go as far as the cemetery – such places were best avoided at night, but I chose this road since I had walked it already that day and so it was familiar; less chance of tripping in the dark and breaking a leg. About halfway to the cemetery, I just lay down by the roadside to take in the beauty of the stars.

After about ten minutes, I heard someone coming along the road, from the direction of the cemetery; they were sobbing. I sat up and as they got closer, I saw that it was Sonia. She was carrying a little wooden cross and a paraffin lamp.

"Sonia, are you okay?" I said, as she approached.

"Ahhh!" she screamed; she hadn't seen me sitting there in the dark.

"It's okay. It's just me, Sandy."

"What are you doing here, sitting alone in the dark?"

She came and sat beside me and held my hand.

"Couldn't sleep. Thinking about stuff, today's events, you. I wish I could leave Rocky here and take you with me!"

"Why don't you just stay here and become a farmer. We could have a good life. Have children. Apparently you and Rocky aren't able to have children."

"Looks that way. We've been together ten years, married for five."

"Who could blame you then, for leaving her?"

I imagined leaving everything behind in Europe – my job, my home with all the comforts I was used to, the whole consumerist society – to come here and live in a very basic village in the Ivory Coast. I looked into her beautiful eyes, which reflected the fire of the paraffin lamp. I wanted to say yes, to truly break away from the destiny I'd been born into, but something – fear, conformism, passivity? – prevented me.

I changed the subject. "What about you? Why were you wandering around in the dark? What's that cross you're carrying?"

"I went to pray for my step-mother, Adèle. By her graveside. You know she died in rather strange circumstances. One minute she was fine, a picture of health, vigorously pilling some rice; then she just fell down dead. She was only forty."

"Heart attack?"

"Well, that's what the nurse said, but a lot of people around here are saying witchcraft was involved."

Here we go again!

"Pray for Adèle's soul, Sandy," urged Sonia.

"I will, I promise."

I found myself kissing her tenderly. Then we just lay there together in the dark, holding hands and looking up at the stars.

It must have been at one or two in the morning when we eventually headed back to our respective rooms. As we exchanged a final embrace I could see tears in her eyes.

Chapter 18

Saint Pedro

The next morning we were back on the road again. There were more tearful farewells, especially between Rocky and her mother, Betty, who was staying on in N'kopé a bit longer. Sonia was there, too. How I wanted to reach out to her, to say come with me, but I couldn't.

We left at about nine a.m., taking another one-hour, bumpy baca ride as far as the bus station in Adzopé. Then it was big buses all the way back to Soubré, changing at Gagnoa as on the outgoing trip. Once at the bus station in Soubré, we found out that the next trip by coach to San Pedro was in two hours time, so we managed to arrange two seats in a *dina* – a slightly newer and less rusty version of the baca. We were promised that it went direct to San Pedro. The journey was 100 km on good tarmac roads, so we were hoping it would take about an hour or so. It took about three hours! We would have been better off waiting for the coach.

The people responsible for the dina could best be described as maverick cowboys, doing everything in their power to get a quick buck. Despite promises of a direct trip, the dina stopped in several villages on the way and in each one they did two or three trips up and down the main street, shouting "San Pedro, San Pedro!" to try and get more people into an already packed dina. They were squeezing five adults into each row, which were already a bit of a squash for four. People in the bus complained, but were just ignored. One old guy made the valid comment, "You only respect money! You don't respect the people that give you the money, your customers… no!"

Then at one point we all had to change to another dina and wait ten minutes or so, while the drivers and their helpers traded money. It was plain that they didn't give a damn about the passengers – even to tell us, "Okay we're going to stop for ten minutes, everyone can get out and take a break." No – instead we had to wait in the hot dina, crammed in like sardines. Still, we eventually got there, just before sunset.

From the bus station we took a taxi to a hotel which was recommended in my guidebook. It no longer existed. The driver recommended us another place, a new hotel called the Marina hotel, in the out-of-town Balmer district, just five minutes walk up from the beach. Thankfully, it was a lovely place: rooms in little bungalows with roofs covered in branches, in the style of village mud huts, but all beautifully plastered and decorated inside. It was fully equipped with TV, shower, air-conditioning... all the mod cons. It was also very cheap: just 12,000 CFA a night.

"Let's go and check out the beach," I suggested to Rocky.

"I'm too tired after the trip," she replied. "You go on. I'm just going to have a shower."

So I wandered down to the deserted beach and took in the beautiful view of the surf against the setting sun. The sand was pure and fine, almost white; here and there, there were massive rocks, smooth and curved with the battering of the waves and the sand. The whole place seemed to have a breathtaking and magical aura about it – the surf formed a fine mist close to the water. I walked, jogged along the beach for twenty minutes or so, and then took a plunge, just taking off my sandals and t-shirt and keeping on my shorts. I had the whole place to myself. Paradise!

When I got back, Rocky had managed to negotiate a meal of grilled fish and rice. Apparently, you usually had to order it in the morning for the evening meal. The food was excellent and so was the service; the guy that served us, Stéphane, was really friendly and told us a little bit about the hotel. It was apparently owned by French people, who were trying to drum up business, hence the reasonable prices. They were competing against other hotels such as the Sophia and the Balmer, which were more expensive four-star joints.

* * *

We stayed four days in San Pedro, making the most of the beach. I went swimming every day; Rocky chickened out, only going for a paddle up to her ankles. To be fair the currents were very strong; even I took care not to go too far out. In the daytime fishermen would take out little sailing boats and use nets to catch fish and crabs. Apart from that we had the beach to ourselves. In such a beautiful relaxing setting, I tried to rekindle our romance; we would walk hand in hand along the beach, but when I kissed her, she would quickly break off, saying, "Let's just keep on walking," or "Let me breathe, Sandy!" Any attempt I made to move towards her in bed was shunned. "I don't feel like it." "I've got a headache." "I'm too tired." The usual excuses.

Despite this, we made the most of our stay in San Pedro. The place definitely had a certain charm. One day we walked to the Motel Balmer, about thirty minute's walk, west, along the coast, at the far end of the Balmer district. It was a class above our little Marina hotel. Very exclusive, with a private beach, a golf course and bungalow rooms, about three times the size of those at the Marina, and no doubt much more luxurious inside. I noticed the prices were about ten times that of the Marina.

Another day we checked out the other hotel by the beach, the hotel Sophia. Another thirty minutes walk, east, towards the town centre. It was the 'in' place, where all the European tourists seemed to hang out, lounging by the pool or on the private beach, with its numbered beach couches. I found it strange that people would prefer to hang out in crowds here, when a few minutes walk away there was a secluded, empty, quiet beach. Again, the room prices were expensive, about four times as much as the Marina. We did have lunch there though – the restaurant was open to non-residents. I sampled crab, presumably caught fresh from the ocean.

Apart from these three hotels, the whole area was kind of

underdeveloped, with just a few rich, white peoples' villas dotted here and there, with high walls, cameras and security guards sitting outside. Near the Marina there was the Italian Consulate's villa; there were also a few large houses being built, some of them very impressive, with curving stairways and pillared terraces. It was rather a strange contrast to see spic and span mansions, with lawns and flowers in front of them, but with bumpy dirt roads leading up to them and surrounded by weeds and *brousse* (wild plants).

To save cash, we ended up trekking quite a bit. We wandered into the town centre, about a forty-five minute walk. There we saw numerous banks, a few interesting artisanal shops, grocery stores, and loads of bars and restaurants – all offering fresh fish and seafood. We explored the *port de pêcheurs* (fishermen's port) with its smelly fish market, and boats of various sizes, ranging from *pirous* (long wooden canoes) to massive transporter ships. We got one of the fishermen to take us on a quick tour of the port in a *pirou*. He was Ghanaian, like a lot of the fishermen there, and supposedly spoke English; but when I tried to have a basic conversation with him, I found that my version of English and his were more or less incompatible. He must have spoken some English dialect, like the French dialect Nouchi. He paddled us right under the biggest cargo ship in the place, and high up above us, we were surprised to see that the crew were all Chinese. They waved at us, shouted greetings, and posed for a photo.

* * *

We decided to leave San Pedro, on Friday the thirteenth of September, and head up to Yamoussoukro. Friday the thirteenth, an unlucky day according to superstition, and that morning I wasn't to be spared. To avoid the same dina debacle as our incoming trip, we decided to go for the big coach option; we found out that there was one direct to Soubré at twelve noon.

From there we could get another direct coach to Yamoussoukro.

So that last morning in San Pedro, I went down to the beach for a final wander and swim. Rocky decided to have a long lie in, so I headed out alone. I took a dip, plunging into the refreshing waves and swimming out as far as I dared, having to use all my strength against the undercurrent to get back to the shore. After lying on a towel to rest and dry myself in the sun, I started to stroll along the beach, to the west.

As I wandered along, I reflected on the history of San Pedro and the Ivory Coast. San Pedro was 'discovered' in the fifteenth century by the Portuguese explorer, Soerire Da Costa, who named it after the patron saint of the day of its 'discovery'. Like many port towns during the colonial period of West Africa, it was used for the transportation of plundered goods: grain, ivory, gold, slaves. Indeed the explorer-merchants, mainly French and Portuguese, named the coasts of that part of West Africa, running from the current Liberia to Nigeria: the Grain Coast, the Ivory Coast, the Gold Coast and the Slave Coast, according to the main type of merchandise traded. Slaves were of course considered a type of merchandise, like any other, at the time. While times had changed, slavery still existed, notably child slavery. I'd already seen the softer form back in Guédéyo. Often migrants were so poorly paid and treated, it could also be considered a form of slavery. It's perhaps telling that the Ivory Coast never bothered to change the country's name or the names of places like San Pedro. The plunder of ivory may have been seriously reduced, due to laws and diminished numbers of elephants, but the cocoa trade – with its use of children and migrants in slavery or near slavery – was in full swing. San Pedro is in fact the number one port in the world for the export of cocoa, picked in part by children and migrant workers. Lost in thought, I suddenly noticed a huge crab, up on the dunes to my right. I went up for a closer look – it was an impressive beast with massive pincers, sitting there impassively – it wasn't moving at all. Was the thing dead? I grabbed a long stick and was just about to poke it in the face to see if it flinched, when I heard a voice behind me: "Watch out, Sandy, those pincers can be dangerous!"

I looked round – it was Rocky. Where did she spring from? Suddenly I felt an excruciating pain in my left hand; the crab had taken advantage of my inattention, scarpered over and pinched into my ring finger and little finger.

"Ahhhhh!" I could feel the pincers digging in. Luckily I was wearing my wedding ring, otherwise the crab would have had my fingers clean off. Rocky quickly grabbed the stick from me and plunged the pointed end right into its head, killing it instantly. The pincers relaxed enough for me to extract my fingers, which were now spurting blood.

"Told you to be careful," said Rocky, wrapping my hand in a clean Lotus handkerchief.

"I would've been fine, if you hadn't crept up on me like that!" I shouted.

I was about to go on castigating her, but we were interrupted by one of the fishermen who'd heard my cries and come running up from his boat, which he'd been about to launch into the ocean.

He pointed at my hand. "You okay? These crabs can be dangerous – shouldn't get too close to their pincers."

"I'm okay, thanks." I replied. Actually I wasn't that okay; I could no longer feel anything in the two fingers which the crab had nipped into.

"That's one big crab! Mind if I take it?" he asked. "Good meat on there."

"Go ahead." At least someone would get something out of this unfortunate incident, another bloody mishap on my Ivoirian adventure.

Once he'd left with the crab, I spoke to Rocky again. "I think I may need stitches. Plus I've lost all sensation in the two fingers. Should probably get it checked out at the nearest hospital."

"I can do the stitching. The sensations will come back

normally, don't worry."

This reminded me of the dog incident. She had patched up the dog-bite professionally and I hadn't caught rabies, so far anyway. I supposed I could trust her to fix up my fingers too.

I let her lead me back to our little hotel bungalow and she deftly put a couple of stitches in each finger and applied sterile dressings. Then we paid for our stay at the hotel reception and headed off for the next stage of our trip – Yamoussoukro.

Chapter 19

Yamoussoukro

Yamoussoukro: the shining jewel of the Ivory Coast, with its presidential palaces, its luxury hotels and golf courses, its huge glistening basilica and of course its lakes and canals and swamps full of crocodiles; or just another mosquito infested hellhole in deepest, darkest Africa? We were about to find out.

Yamoussoukro is the administrative capital of the Ivory Coast; the reason being that it was where the country's first president, Félix Houphouët-Boigny, was born, and he decided he'd continue living there and make it the capital. Hence it was developed from a small village into a modest-sized town. One of his measures during his long presidency, from 1960 to 1993, was to build motorways linking Yamoussoukro to most of the other big towns and cities. So our journey there by bus went smoothly enough, once we got going, away from the anarchy of the bus station in San Pédro. A smooth drive up the motorway in a big coach, for two hours, to Soubré; then another similar coach for about four hours, on more motorway, all the way to Yamoussoukro. There were minimal stops, so we arrived around six thirty p.m. – just as the sun was setting.

We were tired after the journey, so didn't go out that night, but my first impressions of the place – viewed from the bus and then the taxi to the hotel – were good. It looked clean, and well organised – wide avenues and roads all in smooth tarmac; pristine palm-trees, lakes and canals; modern administrative buildings and hotels – all laid out in an efficient grid structure, much like modern American cities.

Our hotel – *Le Jardin* (the garden) – was also a pleasant surprise: spacious bedroom and reception, bar and dining areas all done up like some safari lodge, with stuffed antelope heads and lion and zebra skins hanging from the walls. All spotlessly clean and for about half the price we'd payed for our flea-pit in Abidjan. The restaurant had a wide choice of reasonably priced delicious food. On our first night we both had mouth-wateringly good *poulet yassa*, chicken marinated in spicy lemon sauce, with rice.

The best thing about the place, though, was the breakfast. I've never tasted such great omelettes, made with what must have been eggs just fresh from the chicken, whipped up into a lovely, fluffy, airy texture and just lightly cooked, so that the eggs just melted in your mouth; washed down with beautiful, sweet, freshly squeezed orange juice and freshly ground coffee. In fact, everything seemed so fresh, like it had just been harvested from some luscious Garden of Eden. I think most of it *had* actually been harvested from the hotel's back garden or courtyard, judging by the faint clucking of chickens which could be heard from the restaurant, and what was that other noise? The squealing of pigs? Thankfully, I'd passed on the ham.

So the first morning of our visit, feeling invigorated after such a delicious breakfast, we headed off to visit the Basilica and the presidential crocodiles.

You have to admire the balls of some of these African dictators. This guy Houphouët-Boigny, gets 'voted' in, no opposition, as the first president of the newly independent Ivory Coast in 1960 and just decides that the administrative capital will be transferred from Abidjan to his home town, or rather home village at that time. So by presidential order a big, beautiful, straight motorway is built all the way from Abidjan to Yamoussoukro, all 100 km of it. Huge, white marble, presidential palaces are built surrounded by crocodile filled marshes. And as a finishing touch, a replica of Saint Paul's Basilica in Rome is erected. Strange how local people we talked to were more critical of the Basilica than of the massive presidential palaces. Maybe it's because the palaces were a bit less visible. Hidden behind high walls, and closed to visitors, you had less of an impression of their ostentation; while the Basilica could be admired inside and out, day and night by all and sundry. The beautiful vivid colours of its magnificent stained glass windows were mesmerising. The marble walls and walkways, which stretched out into the savannah, dazzled with their sheer whiteness. Perfectly tuned bells rang loudly out so they could be heard for miles around. The pungent smell of burning incense and the joyous singing and dancing of thousands of worshipers welcomed you as you entered. It was stunning, an enchantment to the senses even to someone like me, coming from Europe. To the poor locals living in shacks and mud huts it must have just been mind blowing. And when you thought about how much it must have cost and what other things the money could have been used for – hospitals, schools, better houses – you began to understand how they felt.

So on the Saturday morning we visited the Basilica: took photos and got people to photograph us standing in front of it, and once inside stared up open-mouthed at the sheer scale of the place, the exquisitely decorated walls and ceilings and the bright colours of the stained glass windows. If you didn't know you were in 20th century Africa, you'd think you were in 6th century Rome, inside a brand new Basilica, just decorated by Michelangelo himself.

Then in the afternoon, after a hearty lunch of attiéké and fish, we went to see the famous presidential crocodiles. They occupied a lake in front of the presidential palace – a moat I suppose you could say; did Houphouët-Boigny assure his long presidency by feeding any disruptive opponents to these crocodiles?

As we got close up to the crocodile enclosure, I was awed: there were about twenty crocodiles, ranging from three to four metres long, with massive jaws. The thin, knee-high, wire fence separating us from these massive monsters seemed derisory. Some of them were basking on a grassy bank on the palace side of the moat, but others were very close to the fence on the side of the moat closest to us. Even more surprisingly, there was a guy in charge of them, a tall, thin, mystical type with a wooden staff, who was inside the enclosure, walking freely amongst them! I presumed they'd just been fed – chicken feathers littered the inside of the enclosure, but still.

There were the ubiquitous Japanese tourists taking photos. We were standing a few feet back from the fence, when one Japanese guy walked in front of us, leaned over the fence and started taking photos of one of the biggest crocodiles, just inches from its head. Suddenly it took a lunge at him! He ducked and it continued on over the fence, jumping on his back and pouncing towards me! Its eyes no longer looked cold and emotionless but fiery and filled with hatred, pure evil! I sprang back but its front teeth just caught my right arm, tearing a big gash on my biceps! A few inches more and it would have had me in its jaws.

Thankfully, the guru attendant sprang quickly into action, beating back the crocodile with his staff before it could attack again. He managed to get it back inside the enclosure, opening a gate and beating it with the stick until it was back inside and he could close the gate again. Then he shouted something at the Japanese guy who'd been taking the photo too close; he was speaking in some language I couldn't understand, Dyula, I think. The Jap just bowed for forgiveness, muttering in Japanese. The guru guy then came over to me and asked, in French, if I was okay.

There was a deep laceration in my arm which was bleeding and I was shaking with shock. "I'll be okay," I stammered.

He gave me a Lotus handkerchief, which I held onto the wound. Then he looked fixedly at Rocky and started shouting, in Dyula again, and pounding his stick on the ground.

Rocky just stared back at him, then said to me, "We'd better go and get your arm fixed up."

She led me off and we flagged down a taxi.

"What was that guy saying to you," I quizzed Rocky in the taxi back to the hotel.

"Oh, nothing much," she replied. "He was just saying, be careful with the tourists. Guy probably lives on tips. If the tourists stop coming, he's got no livelihood."

I was sure there was more to it than that, but didn't press her for more information. As for the dog, the insects/lizards and the crab, she used her nursing skills to bandage me up. I looked like a war casualty with bandages on both arms. Thankfully my left leg and forehead were well on the mend; as was the cut on my right leg, on the thigh where Sonia had scratched me with her nails.

* * *

We stayed on in Yamoussoukro for another four days. My wounds began to heal and I recovered from the shock of almost being eaten alive by a crocodile. I prayed for a full recovery when we went to mass in the Basilica on Sunday. During our stay in Yamoussoukro, we also visited the huge mosque – ornately decorated with colourful mosaics, the Cathedral Saint Augustin – rather plain compared to the exquisite Basilica, and the protestant temple. Houphouët-Boigny hadn't allowed much political opposition, but at least he'd encouraged religious diversity. I didn't come across any chicken-sacrificing animists, though, in Yamoussoukro; maybe all the chickens were used to keep the tourists and the crocodiles well fed.

The day before we left, Tuesday, we went to visit the Hôtel Président. Yet another example of the previous president's exuberance, with its fifteen levels culminating in a huge panoramic restaurant, it dominated the southeast area of the city. We explored its vast complex which included shops, a swimming pool and even a massive golf course. We took the lift up to the panoramic restaurant and the view was stunning – you could see the savannah stretching out for miles. The prices on the menu were also rather startling, the cheapest dish being around 50,000 FCFA. We'd thought about eating there that night, but it was way over our budget, so we headed back into town to the big Maquis Centrale – actually quite a swanky place, with starched white tablecloths and shiny metal cutlery. We tucked into a scrumptious meal of grilled fish and rice, excellent and about a tenth the price of the extortionate Hôtel Président. As we headed back to our hotel through the city centre, we took in the party atmosphere – the smell of grilled kidneys, and the loud music pumping out of ghetto blasters at the various stalls.

"Have you enjoyed your holiday here?" asked Rocky.

"Yes," I replied. "Despite all the various mishaps like being sick or getting attacked by wild animals."

"Yeah, well this is Africa. Wild. Savage. You've got off lightly. Think yourself lucky to be alive."

"Yeah, that crocodile could have dragged me off into the swamp!"

Back at the hotel we packed and went to bed. I'd given up trying to have sex with her. I was becoming less and less attracted by her anyway. This trip hadn't done anything to reduce her waistline, quite the contrary, she'd been stuffing herself with all the delicious Ivorian cuisine and was now fatter than ever. So much for rekindling our marriage.

Chapter 20

Abidjan – Grand Hotel

The next day, it was back on the buses. Another smooth coach trip down the motorway to Abidjan. I spent most of the four hour trip just gazing out the window, taking in the interesting countryside, from wild brush to plantations of banana and palm trees. Who knew when, if ever, I would return to such beautiful exotic scenery.

When we arrived back in Abidjan, the stench and the squalor of the Adjamé slum brought me back to my senses. We got a taxi to the Grand Hotel in Le Plateau district and booked in for the final three nights of the trip. I'd insisted on going to a decent hotel for our last few days in the Ivory Coast; no way was I going back to that dive in Treichville. We took a wander outside that afternoon, then just had dinner at the hotel restaurant, a couple of drinks at the bar then turned in around ten p.m.

* * *

The next day I awoke feeling rather groggy; a rough hangover feel which was strange since I'd only had a couple of beers. I looked at my watch: ten a.m. Had I really slept that long? Rocky wasn't there. I looked around the room and immediately saw that something was wrong. Her case and some of the other bags were missing. I got up, feeling unsteady on my feet. There was a note on the writing desk:

I'm leaving you. Go back to France without me.
  Rocky

I felt the blood rushing to my head. What was going on? She was leaving me? Just like that, on our holiday? No explanation? Was it because I'd slept with Sonia? Who could blame me after about six months of her shunning me. Or had she planned to leave me all along, the trip being her final farewell or a final test which I'd failed? 'Here's where I'm from, where I want to go back to. You could never fit in here. It's over. Goodbye.' Why couldn't she at least have written something like that? I went to the bathroom and splashed cold water on my face. Why did I feel so rough? She must have drugged me, slipping a sleeping tablet in my drink, so she could make a clean getaway.

I quickly got dressed and headed down to the reception; it was too late now for breakfast. They confirmed that she'd left at around six a.m. She hadn't said where she was going. A big, black, chauffeur-driven Mercedes had come to pick her up. What the hell was going on?

Everyone, hotel staff and guests, appeared on edge. There were raised voices, slamming doors; one female guest was crying and being consoled by her husband.

I approached the hotel manager – a fifty-something ebony-skinned man, with short grey hair and moustache, who usually appeared imperturbable. Today he was extremely agitated, sweating profusely and barking orders to his staff.

"What's going on?" I asked. "Is there something wrong?"

"Haven't you heard, sir, there's been an attempted *coup d'état*," he replied. "Didn't you hear the gun-shots during the night?"

"Gun-shots? No!" I exclaimed, not adding that I would have slept through Armageddon, since my wife had drugged me. "Is it over? Is it safe to go out?"

I was thinking of using my remaining two days to try and find out where Rocky had gone, travelling back to Guédéyo if need be, to see if she'd headed back there or if her family knew where she'd gone."

"No, sir. We're strongly advising all our guests to just stay put until things calm down. The whole country is in turmoil, military uprisings in all major cities. Our former president, Robert Guéi, has been killed. It's not safe to go anywhere. Everyplace is shut anyway: shops, restaurants, banks. But don't worry, things will hopefully settle down in a day or two. We'll keep you informed." He clicked his heels together, looked like he was about to salute me, former military guy undoubtedly, but then just nodded, walked off and went back to shouting at his staff.

'A day or two' – that seemed optimistic. I'd read about the previous military coup. The retired general Guéi hadn't led the rebellion but had been called out of retirement to briefly take over power. There had been riots, mayhem and overall instability in the country for about a year, until the current president, Laurent Gbagbo, had been elected, and had ended up having to use violence to oust Guéi. The latter had fled but remained on the political scene until his assassination that night. Numerous questions came to mind. Had Guéi been involved in the coup today? Would Gbagbo manage to quell the rebellion and get things back to normal? How long was I going to be stuck here? Would I make my return flight in two days? How could I find out what had happened to Rocky, why she'd left me so abruptly? And if I did make my flight on Saturday, did I really want to leave here not knowing what her game was?

There was a big queue for the reception lobby telephone cabin; the rates were about half those of calling from your room. I decided to just use the phone back in my room anyway, to try and get hold of Rocky's parents. This could take a while, since it would involve calling a phone booth in Soubré and getting the owner to pass on a message via the baca-boys, to be there at a certain hour or else call me back. Before calling, I checked on my money and papers – passport, credit cards and all the remaining money was there. Rocky had apparently left with just the small amount of cash that she kept in her own wallet; I always took care of the bulk of the cash. She'd even left her own credit card, linked to our joint account. What message was she sending? I no longer need you or your money. Heading off in a chauffeur-driven Merc – had she ditched me for someone richer? A lot richer apparently.

I called the booth in Soubré and asked the booth owner to get the message to André or Betty – be at the booth for a call the next day at twelve noon. The booth owner said he'd try. Didn't I know there was a civil war on?

* * *

I spent the rest of the day following events on TV, or down in the restaurant or bar: alcohol – always a solution to take the edge off things. That Thursday night, most of the other patrons sat around tables in couples or small groups, fretting about the events. I was alone at the bar apart from one other guy, so after an initial beer and a whisky I struck up a conversation with him.

"Terrible events, eh?" I opened.

"Sshyeah, bloody Africa," he slurred apparently quite far gone. "Godforsaken place." He was white, dark brown hair, early thirties, maybe a couple of years older than me, and like me, looked a bit the worse for wear. His left arm was in a plaster, his right eye was covered with bandages and there was a recently healed scar running half the length of his right forearm. *And was that a Scottish accent I detected?*

"Where you from?"

"Shhhcotland, mate. Glasgae. Andy. Pleasshed ta meet ye'!"

"Sandy. Good to meet you. I'm Scottish too, would you believe. Dundee."

We shook hands, both wincing from our respective wounds.

"Shoo whit brings ye' tae Ivory Coassht, pal?"

"Visiting my wife's family. She's from here, but we live in France." I was still in denial of the fact that she'd left me.

"Poor sod! I'm married to an Ivoirian lass too, Gabriella. Or should I say was married. I'm getting out now, while I can. Nightmare. Leaving her and this mad country."

Andy and Gabriella? I thought back to those bizarre happenings at University. I looked more closely at his face, trying to remember the photo I'd seen of Andy, the convent janitor's son. Was it him?!

"Does your dad work as a janitor at a convent in Royston? Dave? And your mum's Shona?"

"Yeah, thatsh them. Or was them. They're both deceased now. Rest in peace. Did ye know them?"

"Ah, sorry to hear that. Sincere condolences. I did know them, yes. Met them when I was studying at Strathclyde. Around the time of that fire that burnt down the convent. Also met a nun called Bernadette. She had some strange stuff to say about your Gabriella."

"Yeah, long story. Should have listened to her, even if she was a bit crazy." He looked down at his now empty glass.

"What you drinking? Let me get you a refill." I'd buy him refills all night if he could shed some light on Gabriella, Bernadette and her warnings.

"Whisky."

I signalled to the barman to give him another whisky and got one for myself. I also ordered a couple of bottles of the local Flag beer to wash them down. We chinked glasses and sipped some of the whisky and the beer.

"So, tell me what happened back at the convent. Your parents said it was just an accident."

"It was no accident. It was Gabriella. I know that now."

"How could it have been? She wasn't even there."

His eyes glazed over – was he recalling the events or was the booze getting the better of him? Apparently both, because he shuddered, uttering "Oh God! It's so terrible what she's done!" Then he downed the rest of the whisky before slumping into unconsciousness, his head resting on his hands on top of the bar.

Damn! I should have got him a coke.

I tried shaking him to get him to wake up, but it was no use.

He was comatose. I eventually had to get the barman to help me carry him back to his room. We just left him fully clothed on top of the bed.

* * *

Despite my hangover the next morning, I made it down for breakfast at around nine a.m. The mood of the place seemed a bit less uptight than the previous day; the news on the TV filled me in on the reason for this: the rebels had failed to take Abidjan or any of the major cities except Bouaké, Ivory Coast's second largest city, way up in the north. There was no sign of Andy, so after eating I enquired at reception if he'd surfaced yet?

"Oh yes, sir," said the cheery female receptionist. "He left by taxi for the airport this morning at six a.m. It's now open again. Most of the flights are back on. Abidjan is getting back to normal." She beamed.

Great! Just when I thought I might be able to shed some light on Bernadette, African witchcraft and so on, the guy with all the answers pisses off on an early flight. How had he managed to sober up so quickly, given the state he was in the previous night and what was it about this place and people heading off at six in the morning? At least I would be able to get my flight as planned the next day. But did I really want to leave without finding out what happened to Rocky?

I tried calling the booth in Soubré again at twelve noon, but as I had feared the owner had been unable to get the message to Rocky's parents.

"Sorry, sir, but it's war! Abidjan might be getting back to normal, but up here there are still skirmishes; people getting arrested, killed or worse; road blocks everywhere. Public transport is limited or non-existent. I'll keep trying, but it will probably be days or weeks even before any baca will be going to Guédéyo."

"I have to leave tomorrow," I replied. I'd made my decision. I was getting my flight the next day. There was no way I was going looking for Rocky in this war-torn country. Even if there had been no war, I think I would have left. My flight was non-modifiable, non-refundable and my visa was about to run out – did I want to become a 'sans papiers' in the Ivory Coast? The ultimate irony. Plus I had to get back to my job, or they'd probably fire me. No. It was time to go.

"Can you please get them to call me back in France," I requested the booth owner. "It's important. Anytime after ten p.m. tomorrow." I gave him my home phone number and my work number in France.

* * *

Abidjan might have been getting back to normal, but I didn't venture out that day. I didn't feel like drinking or socialising, so I just moped around my room and did my packing. As I flung things into my case, I came across the rosary beads Bernadette had given me all those years ago. I'd kept them with me all this time, but hadn't really used them to pray much. Maybe I should have. Maybe I should have listened to her advice and I wouldn't have ended up like this. I picked up the beads and said a decade of the rosary, before putting them back in the case. Too little, too late?

The next day, Saturday, it was my turn to check out of the hotel at six a.m. I left the troubled country of Ivory Coast, catching my flight as planned, back to Paris – via Zurich, as on the departure flight.

Epilogue

I never heard from Rocky again. What little contact I had with her family – the odd phone call or email – didn't get me much further forward as to why she'd left me so abruptly or where the hell she was now. They said that they hadn't heard from her either, that she'd just disappeared.

Something about her having moved to Germany. But that was just a rumour, no precise places or names of people she might be with or what she might me doing.

One night, about three months after she'd left I had the recurring nightmare of the infinite writhing ball of filth, except this time it was worse; this time there was blood, living things being crushed or cut up, and worst of all the cries of a baby. I awoke feeling nauseous, with the sensation of a lump in my stomach, my heart beating fast, as if I'd been running, trying but failing to prevent something terrible from happening. I also felt a terrible, inexplicable sadness.

* * *

This feeling of sadness then stayed with me. I struggled to just carry out every day actions like getting up, eating, and working. But the months and years went by and I eventually got my life back together. I divorced Rocky after about four years' absence; three years was the legal minimum; I allowed an extra year, then I gave her up for dead. I wished she was dead, instead of leaving me in doubt like this, but deep down I knew she was still alive.

I kept very little contact with her family. Even if it wasn't justified I felt they were guilty by association. At one point, maybe about five years after our fateful trip and her disappearance, her Aunt Claire called and after the usual pleasantries – how are you, how's the family – she dropped the bombshell that she'd heard from Rocky. Apparently she'd remarried, to some rich, German industrialist, and was living it up in some castle in Bavaria! Claire didn't give me the details, I don't think she had much more information as to the exact place she was living or the name of her new husband. *Rocky you gold grabbing bitch*, I thought to myself. You could've at least called me. What are you hiding? I had this feeling not just that she'd used me, but that there was some dark secret, I couldn't quite uncover.

* * *

The years passed. I stayed on in France, only going back home to Scotland now and again, to visit my family and the few friends I'd kept in touch with. I went looking for Andy, but couldn't find any trace of him. As for Gabriella, my Gabriella, I never saw her again either, but I did meet her brother, Michael, by chance on one of my visits back to Dundee. He confirmed that she had indeed gone back to Kenya after completing her studies in medicine. She'd become a surgeon no less and was married to another Kenyan surgeon.

"No children," he mentioned. "But they seem happy enough like that. Doing really well for themselves."

No children. Strange coincidence. Just like me and Rocky.

Rocky. Not knowing what she'd done had left me damaged: agitated, unable to concentrate on matters at hand, unable to commit to anything or anyone. I got by on short-term employment and even shorter term relationships, the ever present feeling of loss / of something missing hanging over me. About 13 years after she'd gone I was wandering around the 13th arrondissement of Paris, checking out some Chinese stores, and by chance I bumped into Sarafin, Claire's current husband; she'd divorced from Zeus way back, remarried Sarafin and had more kids.

"Hey, Sandy! Ayoka! How are you?"

His face had hardly aged since I saw him 13 years ago, but now he walked rather slowly and hesitantly as if he had a back injury.

"So, so, you know, life goes on. How about you and Claire and the family?"

"We're all fine. Family's growing, four kids now." He paused and gave a nervous cough. "Yeah. That Rocky. She always was a terrible one. We hardly hear from her." He sensed my discomfort on bringing up the subject of Rocky and looked down at the ground. Looking up again, he asked, "Why don't you come around for lunch on Sunday? We'll have a chat, catch up. You can meet the kids."

I didn't have anything better to do and maybe this would at last be the chance to find out about Rocky. "Okay. That would be nice."

* * *

I arrived on the following Sunday at around midday. I'd called Sarafin when I arrived at the train station nearest their house: Corbeil-Essonnes, far out in the Parisian suburbs. He arrived in about five minutes in a battered old Peugot 206 and drove me to their dwelling. They lived in an *HLM* (council flat) in a small block of flats, which seemed to be in a better neighbourhood than they lived in before – the infamous Tarterets, with its filthy high-rise flats, burnt-out cars and drug-dealers, where even the police fear to venture, let alone pizza-delivery.

There was the smell of rice and sauce cooking, making my mouth water before I even got into the apartment. Claire was doing the eldest girl's hair. I presumed it was Lady – yes that was her actual first name. I hadn't seen her since she was a toddler. The three younger children in the family were also present, all sitting on the living room couch.

"Hi, Claire! How are you?" We kissed in the French style, four times, twice on each cheek, as if no time had passed since the twenty years when we first met. I handed over a box of chocolates and a bottle of soda; I'd long since given up drinking.

"Waah! You have totally changed." She took in my receding hairline and the white in my beard and remaining hair. "You're showing your age."

"Thanks. We all get old and decrepit. Such is life," I chipped in cheerfully.

"So, you remember Lady?" She gestured to the young girl sitting on the ground, with her hair half done. Claire was sitting on the sofa just behind her and continued doing her hair as we talked.

I crouched down and gave the usual kisses greeting. Lady smiled shyly and self-consciously in that teenager way.

"Good to see you again," I said to her. "You were just a little kid when I saw you last."

Then I looked at the second eldest of the kids assembled. "And you must be, Yoni, I take it? You were just a baby."

"And these are the last two, Jonas and Gandy. I don't think you ever met them." Sarafin gestured to the last two kids on the sofa, who looked around eight and five respectively.

More kisses all round, then they sat me down at the table and we chatted about this and that. How's the family, how's your work, who's got married or divorced, who's had more kids...

"What about Timothée?" I enquired. This was Claire's first son, whom she had with her previous husband, Zeus, the guy she was with when I met her, twenty years ago. He would be in his twenties by now. I'd heard that he'd done a few months in prison for beating up some policemen; that's what happens in the 'Tarterets'.

"Oh, he's fine. He lives with his dad." End of subject.

After a while we all sat at the table and had the rice and gumbo sauce. It was delicious as usual. There was some pork, too, but I declined; I'd more or less given up meat.

"So, clean living eh?" said Sarafin, guzzling on a bottle of cheap beer.

"Yes, well, you know, keep healthy and all that," I replied meekly.

The taste of the sauce, and just seeing Claire again and hearing her voice took me back years and I could almost imagine Rocky sitting there, too, joking away.

"I suppose you don't smoke either?" enquired Sarafin.

"Eh, no." I'd never really smoked, but I remembered back in the day, we'd shared the odd joint together on the balcony of their flat in the 'Tarterets' housing scheme.

He went outside and when he came back in, he'd obviously been on the wacky backy and not just normal cigarettes. He swayed a little when he walked and his pupils seemed more dilated. I decided this was the perfect time to finally get some more information on Rocky and on what really went on during our trip back in 2002. "So do you get back to the home country much, Sarafin?"

"Yes, now and then. I go back at least once a year. I'd like to set up a business there. Then maybe we could move back."

"What, like to retire?"

"Hmmf." Claire snorted. "No way." She'd gone back to doing Lady's hair. The intricate pleats and tresses of African hair-dos can take up to two days. The three other kids had gone off to play video games in one of the bedrooms.

"Yes, well she's quite happy here; never goes back." Sarafin sighed. "But home's best. France is tough. If you have a little money, you can set up a small business over there, say, selling clothes, and live the good life. Here it's impossible with all the taxes and charges."

"What, don't you have to pay tax over there?"

"Everyone does what he wants."

I took that as a no. "Tell me one thing, Sarafin, Claire... have you heard from Rocky?" I finally blurted out the question I'd been dying to ask.

They looked at each other knowingly. "She's more or less deserted the family. Just calls her parents now and again. Oh, and sends back loads of money; although we've never seen any of it. Just to her parents and her sisters. Her dad's the village leader now, back in Ottawa," Claire said.

So, he'd finally grasped the village chief's power.

"Ah yes, Ottawa, remember it like it was yesterday. André that wily old dog. So how'd he manage to take over?"

"The old chief got arrested back in 2011. There was an uprising of immigrants – you know, all the Burkinabés and Maliens and so on, supported by the FRCI, Ouattara's rebel forces. No sons to takeover, so André, second in command, got to become chief," explained Claire.

"The FRCI even killed several people, including Kouadjo Krobou, remember him, the village idiot?" said Sarafin. "How could they? Kouadjo wouldn't hurt a fly."

"Kouadjo, yeah, I remember him well. May he rest in peace," I said solemnly. Death by the 'commandos' – had he foreseen his violent death all this time? His rantings apparently weren't so crazy after all.

"Anyway, what about Rocky?" I got back onto the main reason I'd come here. "Where the hell is she? What was all that about marrying some rich Bosch?"

"The guy was visiting the Ivory Coast, to oversee the modernisation and expansion of that palm-oil factory near Ottawa, and apparently Rocky seduced him and then he took her back to Germany. He's minted – a billionaire. Owns most of the palm-oil factories in the Ivory Coast and elsewhere in the world," Sarafin explained. "We don't know where she lives, somewhere in Bavaria. I think her sister, Geraldine, might have been to visit her once, in their massive castle, hidden away somewhere in the Black forest."

Bitch! I murmured under my breath. I'd obtained a little more information, but wasn't much further forward. I could try contacting Geraldine perhaps; she still lived in the Paris region as far as I knew.

"What was all that crap about witches and witches' lists? It was pretty weird when I was over there in 2002, people got sick, some even died..."

"Witches, black magic, offerings to the devil... it's all true. You have to watch out. The most powerful magic is when the witch offers some sacrifice." Sarafin's eyes lost focus, as if he was imagining some horrific scene.

"What you mean animals? Not humans surely?"

"Yes. Humans. And if they're close to you, a brother, a sister, a child, the magic is all the stronger. The witch can gain immense power," he said ominously.

"I see. You don't think Rocky's dad was involved? I remember he almost got lynched while we were out there... and now he's the village chief."

"Who knows, maybe him, maybe one of his wives, or maybe they just paid the witch. Ah yes, that's Africa for you: black magic, mysterious deaths, corruption."

Yes, and you want to go back there? I felt like saying, but held my tongue.

We changed the subject, got onto safer ground: football, work, politics... but I was brooding on what they'd said about witches. I knew somehow, deep down, that I was mixed up in all this.

After lunch and a couple of hours chatting, I made my excuses and left. Sarafin said to come back anytime, but I doubted I would. Being with them brought back too many memories.

* * *

The next morning, back at my flat, I was putting a novel I'd just read on the bookcase and as I rearranged the books, I chanced upon the guidebook I'd brought along on our trip to the Ivory

Coast. I flipped through it, looking at some of the brochures, postcards, menus and hotel business cards I'd put in, souvenirs of the places we'd visited. Looking at the map, I traced out with my finger the route we'd taken. The main places we'd stayed at, in order, were as follows: Abidjan, Ottawa (near Soubré), N'Koupé (near Adzopé), San Pedro, Yamoussoukro, then back to Abidjan. I didn't really think about it at the time, but now it occurred to me that it was a rather strange itinerary we'd taken. Okay, when we were in Ottawa we'd had to cross the whole country, practically, to get to a funeral in N'Koupé; but after that why did we swing back over to San Pedro, followed by Yamoussoukro, and not the inverse, which would have been a lot shorter? Then suddenly I saw it. The route traced out a pentagram! *Look for the sign which the witch has made to the devil,* the old woman in the forest had said, *preferably with blood.* The blood must have been my blood, spilled at each corner of the pentagram! Oh God, Rocky! What have you done? It was you that led me on that route!

I felt my heartbeat increasing, a lump forming in my throat and my eyes filled with tears. I dropped the book and stumbled to the bathroom, to rinse my face. In my anger and confusion, I kicked out and the piece of wood panelling under the sink, just below the little cupboard, fell off. I got down on my hands and knees to see if I could put it back on, and saw something which had been hidden behind the panel. I reached down and got it out. It was a small bottle of red food colouring. What the hell was that doing down there? It must have been Rocky that had hidden it.

And then it hit me. Red food colouring, hidden below the cupboard where she kept her tampax. She'd been faking her periods. She'd been pregnant when we went to the Ivory Coast! *Human sacrifice!* Oh no, Rocky! What have you done to our child? And for what? So your father could become village chief? So you could marry someone rich and powerful? ROCKY YOU BITCH! YOU WITCH! I'M GOING TO FIND YOU. YOU'RE ON MY LIST NOW AND I'M GOING TO KILL YOU!

COSMIC
EGG
BOOKS

If you prefer to spend your nights with Vampires and Werewolves rather than the mundane then we publish the books for you. If your preference is for Dragons and Faeries or Angels and Demons – we should be your first stop. Perhaps your perfect partner has artificial skin or comes from another planet – step right this way. Our curiosity shop contains treasures you will enjoy unearthing. If your passion is Fantasy (including magical realism and spiritual fantasy), Horror or Science Fiction (including Steampunk), Cosmic Egg books will feed your hunger.

If you have enjoyed this book, why not tell other readers by posting a review on your preferred booksite. Recent bestsellers from Cosmic Egg Books are:

The Zombie Rule Book, A Zombie Apocalypse Survival Guide
Tony Newton
The book the living-dead don't want you to have!
Paperback: 978-1-78279-334-2
e-book: 978-1-78279-333-5

Cryptogram, Because the Past is Never Past
Michael Tobert
Welcome to the dystopian world of 2050, where three lovers are haunted by echoes from eight-hundred years ago.
Paperback: 978-1-78279-681-7
e-book: 978-1-78279-680-0

Purefinder
Ben Gwalchmai
London, 1858. A child is dead; a man is blamed and dragged through hell in this Dantean tale of loss, mystery and fraternity.
Paperback: 978-1-78279-098-3
e-book: 978-1-78279-097-6

600ppm, A Novel of Climate Change
Clarke W. Owens
Nature is collapsing. The government doesn't want you to know why. Welcome to 2051 and 600ppm.
Paperback: 978-1-78279-992-4
e-book: 978-1-78279-993-1

Creations
William Mitchell
Earth 2040 is on the brink of disaster. Can Max Lowrie stop the
self-replicating machines before it's too late?
Paperback: 978-1-78279-186-7
e-book: 978-1-78279-161-4

The Gawain Legacy
Jon Mackley
If you try to control every secret, secrets may end up
controlling you.
Paperback: 978-1-78279-485-1
e-book: 978-1-78279-484-4

Mirror Image
Beth Murray
When Detective Jack Daniels discovers the journal of female
serial killer Sarah he is dragged into a supernatural world,
where people's dark sides are not always hidden.
Paperback: 978-1-78279-482-0
e-book: 978-1-78279-481-3

Moon Song
Elen Sentier
Tristan died too soon, Isoldé must bring him back to finish his
job... to write the Moon Song.
Paperback: 978-1-78279-807-1
e-book: 978-1-78279-806-4

Origin
Colleen Douglas
Fate rarely calls on us at a moment of our choosing.
Paperback: 978-1-78279-492-9
e-book: 978-1-78279-491-2

Perception
Alaric Albertsson
The first ship was sighted over St. Louis...and then St. Louis was gone.
Paperback: 978-1-78279-261-1
e-book: 978-1-78279-262-8

Find more titles and sign up to our readers' newsletter at http://www.johnhuntpublishing.com/fiction.

Follow us on Facebook at https://www.face-book.com/JHPfiction and Twitter at https://twitter.com/JHPFiction.

Most titles are published in paperback and as an e-book. Paperbacks are available in physical bookshops. Both print and e-book editions are available online. Readers of e-books can click on the live links in the titles to order.